RAMSHACKLE

RAMSHACKLE

Elizabeth Reeder

FREIGHT BOOKS

First published in the UK April 2012
By Freight Books
49-53 Virginia Street
Glasgow, G1 1TS
www.freightbooks.co.uk

A CIP catalogue reference for this book is available from the British Library

ISBN 978 0 9566135 7 8

FT
Pbk

Typeset by Freight in Plantin

Printed and bound in the Czech Republic

the publisher acknowledges investment from
Creative Scotland toward the publication of this book

Elizabeth Reeder, originally from Chicago, lives in Scotland. Her writing has been published in anthologies and journals including *The Kenyon Review*, *Chapman*, *PN Review*, and *Gutter Magazine*, and has been broadcast on BBC Radio 4. She teaches on the Creative Writing Programme at University of Glasgow. You can find out more at **ekreeder.com**

For FGR

FRIDAY

We're sitting at the kitchen table. It's late. Our mugs of tea have gone cold. I pick my nose when dad looks down at the key in his hands and I stick the winter-dry booger under the table like it's gum. Then I move to the side, away from him, from the booger he doesn't even notice. He's telling me the story of Old Mrs Morse's big old oak door and he's talking about making a key that'll do the door justice. I'm thinking about whether or not I should have sex with Quiz.

He walks over and turns the heat down. I imagine the cold seeping in from the windows. He returns and stretches out a hand, pulls me up and into a hug. 'Time for bed, Roe.'

'Aren't we going to read?'

'You're too old for that, aren't you?'

And I am, have been for years, but he smiles and I go upstairs. When I get into bed he spreads out at my feet, on the comforter, and even though I've already read the entire trilogy myself, I open the first book and read from the place he fell asleep last time. Lyra is trying to figure out how to read the alethiometer. Night fills the room with the creaking of branches and the wind, and my dad falls asleep on my bed while I'm reading. After a while I reach over, turn off the light and listen to him breathe.

SATURDAY

When I wake up, it's cold and quiet. Downstairs there's day old coffee in the pot. Dad's not here so I turn the heat back up. His boots, gloves and old heavy oilskin coat are gone. It's twenty-four below with windchill and he's wise to have wrapped up. There's no answer on his cell but I leave a message. I get dressed, crack open his bedroom door. His bed hasn't been slept in. We're supposed to be making an early start at the shop this morning but when I call, there's no answer there either.

The car's still in the garage. Where the hell is he?

I wrap up and walk into town. Carl's in the diner. I hand him an insulated mug and order a latte, two sugars, to go.

'That stuff'll stunt your growth. How about a hot chocolate, Roe?'

'Look at me, coach is already after me to join the girl's basketball team.' Carl starts to make a hot chocolate anyway.

'You can never be too tall,' he stands up straight, grins.

'You're not fifteen.'

He adds an extra spoonful of chocolate. 'Are you opening the shop for your old man?' he asks.

'Not exactly,' I run my hand along the edge of the counter. 'Have you seen him this morning?'

'Nope,' Carl raises an eyebrow as he hands me my mug.

'Thanks Carl,' I say and slide off the stool.

'Roe,' he shouts after me, but I've gone by then.

I wipe the frost from my dad's shop window with my glove. Peer in. It's dark and empty. I try the door handle. Knock. Try it again, shake it a bit. He's not here. Missing work, not opening the shop early on a Saturday for all the anxious errand-runners, that's just not like dad at all.

We have a pact. I call and say where I am, he does the same. It's an agreement we made a few years ago, when I badgered him into dropping my curfew.

'It's about courtesy and responsibility,' I argue.

'Is that so?' he says, 'I thought it was about you being home by 10:30.'

'It's about knowing where I am.'

I put on my I-can-do-no-wrong face.

'I'm not going to make a decision simply because you look like an angel. You forget, I know your foibles.'

'So what are my foibles?'

Inconsistent time-keeping is at the top of his list but he drops the curfew anyway and I call home if I'm going to be out later than we've agreed. He's done the same for me. Until today.

Back at home I turn up the phone ringer to full volume, put my cell in my back pocket on vibrate, take my hot chocolate and sit on the couch and listen to Car Talk. The brothers are just being the brothers, with automobile in-jokes and callers who imitate the death rattles of their cars for the benefit of us listeners. How can you help but laugh? From this point on the couch, I can see the lake and the TV (if it was on) at the same time. The weather is bitter and wild and the lake, far out beyond the stretch of shore-ice, whips itself up into froth. Like the coffee Carl won't let me have.

The couch is a wreck. We wear it hard and it's fraying where Dad's legs stretch to the table and where my feet fold under me and I play with the cord edging with my fingers. I usually have to fight with dad over this spot. It's like a chain reaction—if you do the dishes, you lose the couch. Double loser. Or, heaven forbid, I finally win and then have to go to the bathroom, he steals the couch right back. Like a kid.

Today it's all mine. But I don't stay sitting for long, in a flash I'm up and in and out of the rooms. The radio is loud. I'm fidgety, half-heartedly picking up the house. His stuff is everywhere. As I clean, I pile his locks and keys and shoes and tools and papers and books and half-finished projects by his workbench.

He's still not here. On the radio Ira Glass starts talking about how you

3

can't choose the moments that change your life and I'm thinking, of course you can. The way my dad tells the story of getting me, it's like I chose him. Not the other way around.

I wipe down the inside panes of all the windows. I vacuum upstairs and downstairs, clean the kitchen floor and look out the clean windows every time I pass by. I make a huge bowl of pan-popped popcorn with half a stick of melted butter poured over it and nibble on it through the day. And eat Hershey's chocolate with almonds. And an apple. And then an orange. I drink Coke like it's going out of style. There's a film over my teeth and so, when I clean the bathroom, I give them a good scrub and floss too.

It's not like it's the first time I've been alone in the house. Sometimes dad stays over at Steve's if they've been to a jazz club or at the Green Mill, or if a Cubs game runs into extra innings and he doesn't want to make the trip north, he'll stay with Linden. But he always gives me warning, I always know where he is.

I wrap up warm and walk across to Old Mrs Morse's house. The frost on the windows is thick. A chunk of sandstone has broken off a buttress and fallen through a drift. Dad needs to take care of this. Like water dissolving a sugarcube, the weather is eating into the old place. The black roof, so defiant against the sky, rests on the brick wall, the white snow.

What's black and white and red all over?

A newspaper.

Her house: heritage red, innocent white, witches' black.

Beyond the edge of the ravine, down past the tree roots and dirt-sand-ice, a short flat width of sandy snow morphs into the ice of Lake Michigan. Letting my heels take the weight of each step, I follow the path down to the beach. My legs burn with cold. My nose hairs freeze. So do my ears despite my hat pulled down low. I struggle back up the path and there's the house, growing lighter as the sky grows dark. I kick the tips of my boots against the top step to knock off the snow, turn the handle and push the door with my shoulder in one quick, smooth action. I warm up my hands and thighs by sitting on the radiator in the family room. My ears puff up and burn because I left my earrings in and the metal conducted the cold right through them.

Downstairs is this sort of open plan: kitchen, breakfast room, family room, dad's workspace. Counterclockwise around a square-faced clock. I sit on the radiator and look at all of his things. The new pile I've made today. Where the hell is he?

My butt vibrates. Like a jackhammer. I flip the phone open. It's Jess. Bad-girl Jess.

'Hiya,' I say, voice light as anything.

'I just got up. Wondering if you're going to Lucy's party tonight.'

'I don't think so Jess.'

'Come on square. Kevin's going to bring a keg. Jason will be there.'

She's been trying to set me up with Jason since forever. The footballers. The 'in' crowd. My beautiful Quiz, in her mind, is quixotic; he's not good enough for me and his rugby biceps don't impress her.

'No can do. Loads to do.'

'I don't believe you.'

And with good reason.

'Gotta go Jess. See you tomorrow? Only you can make doing those stupid maps bearable.'

'Sure thing. Call me,' and her voice is already distant, her finger pressing the next number. I'm usually her first call, but by no means her last.

When it gets dark outside I flick on the front porch light, hoping it might be a beacon. The radio simply isn't enough. On goes the TV. That's not enough either. I call Quiz.

'Berg residence.'

'Hey there, babes.'

'Hey.' His voice softens from neutral, to me. 'Whatcha doing?'

'Nothing. You?'

'Nothing.'

'Wild out there.'

'Yup.'

'You have practice today?' I think about Quiz in his rugby gear, his muscles.

'Yup. What have you been doing?'

'Watching TV all day.' And it's when I lie to him, when I don't tell him about my dad not coming home that shit kicks in. I keep my voice steady. 'Gotta go. Wanna come over after practice tomorrow?'

'Sure.'

I'm sitting and staring at my dad's junk. I wouldn't even know where to start to look to find his address book. The CTA train guide to the 'El' right on the top. As if he needs that.

Davis is next.

In the direction of travel, doors open on the right at Davis.

Around nine the wind dies down and the house is loud with sound, creaking and settling. I check and recheck the windows and doors. I walk through the house with a blanket over my shoulders; I remind myself of Old Mrs Morse as she paced her way through her last few years in her house next door. The lake is quiet, the ice too thick, too far out to let the water near the beach.

Near midnight the wind picks up again and I phone Linden. I don't want to. But, despite myself, I'm a bit nervous of the walls and windows as they rattle in the wind, and I remember the time we were locked out when I was a kid, how dad wrenched the window of the basement open so I could crawl through and open the door from the inside. If we can do it, so can someone else.

Aunt Linden answers. She's out of breath like she's run for the phone.

'Linden, it's me, Roe.'

'Roe?' Her voice has a touch of annoyance until she realizes that I'd only phone at this time of night if something was up. 'What's wrong Roe?'

All day I've been calm. Thinking he's just popped out for errands. Or just forgot to tell me about a meeting or something.

'Do you know where dad is?' It should feel like relief but somehow asking makes all the fear I feel real.

'I've not heard from him. Is he late coming home from a night with Steve? Maybe they went to a club on the southside?'

'I've not seen him since last night.' My voice breaks into a thousand pieces.

'Roe?'

I'm thinking, he's left me, he's gone. I don't know why but I'm thinking that he's gotten tired of looking after me. He was really pissed off last week when I asked if Quiz could sleep over. I push him too far. I'm thinking he's left because my room is always a mess.

'Roe… Honey? I'll be there as soon as I can. Turn on the lights. Make us some coffee. We'll figure out where he is. Don't you worry.'

I turn on the lights. Turn up the heat too. It's freezing and the wind tears through the place. As if Old Mrs Morse's house was the only one needing attention. This place is standing but swaying. Solid, but in need of our yearly lick of paint. All of the locks are in top shape but some good that does when you could hit the frames and knock the windows in easy.

I'm on my second cup by the time Linden gets here. I see her through the kitchen window and her Ugg boots work just fine on the hardened, icy drive. They compress the layer of new, dry snow. All that crackling makes it sound like she's walking on Styrofoam. She's just like my dad but in a girl's body. I'm nearly as tall as her now. Her big coat hides the sins of her dressing gown and pjs and when she hugs me that's when I know exactly what I think and burst into tears. It's ridiculous. We can't even call the police because it's not been forty-eight hours. And here I am a basket case. I should know better. For fuck sake.

I pull away. Wipe my eyes with my sleeves.

'Don't you worry Roe. He'll be home soon.'

Linden takes off her boots and pulls socks out of her coat pocket before she takes it off too.

'What's in the bag?'

'My work clothes.'

'Charlie still back at yours?'

'Who's Charlie?' She cracks a grin and we both know that she left someone, if not Charlie, behind in her apartment.

'I shouldn't be drinking coffee this late.' She holds the mug close to her face, closes her eyes.

Her guard is up and down at the same time. True worry agitating next to an easy sense of what needs to be done. We both sit.

'Tell me about last night. Today.'

Panic. Relief. Caffeine rush. Exhaustion. Absolute opposites. A fear that he's left me, and complete belief he'll walk through that door at any minute.

We drink coffee, feet up on our chairs and anyone would have thought we were sisters. But we're not sisters, this isn't a slumber party, and when we sleep together in my bed, it's Linden who turns off the lights, who holds me as I cry myself to sleep.

THE NIGHT BEFORE
THE DAY AFTER

I see us at the table on Friday night. I pick my nose and I put the booger under the table like it's gum. Then I move to the side, away from him. Maybe he shifts closer to me again. Maybe. But I think that's me adding something to the memory that just didn't happen. He's telling me the story of Old Mrs Morse's ancient door, worrying a key in his hand.

I replay the image again and again. It feels like a memory I've always had, but it's only a day old. I see the scene: the table, the keys he's working on, the book I'm pretending to read, and I see it: he looks down so as not to cry. I wipe my snot under the table and move away. It is too much, me moving away from him. He wants to say, 'I have something to find out, something to find. It's important.' He wants to say this and knows he can't. He stands up and when he hugs me goodnight, it takes every ounce in his body not to squeeze me tight, not to have his grasping hands leave marks on my arms. His hug is simple, everyday.

'Aren't we going to read?'

'You're too old for that, aren't you?'

And I am, have been for years, but he smiles and when I get into bed he spreads out at my feet, on the comforter. I'm reading aloud, it's a cold January night, and the lake has frozen for the first time this season. Branches brush against the window and my dad falls asleep on my bed while I'm reading, and when I wake in the morning he's gone.

SUNDAY

There's snow everywhere when I get up. From my bedroom window I see huge whorls of white drifting out on the lake. Linden's car is snowed in. A dog's pissed against her bumper and the electric yellow has burned small wormholes down to a layer of ice that won't melt.

Downstairs, Linden is sitting on the floor in the living room. A sketch book and photographs and small etching plates scattered about.

'Afternoon, sleepy head.'

'It's not…' But I see the clock and it's just after noon. 'Why didn't you get me up?'

'Where's the fire? What harm's a bit of sleep?' She gets up off the floor. 'Pancakes?'

She's already made the Bisquick batter and it's got hard edges because she made it hours ago.

'What time did you get up?'

'It's been a while anyway.'

She avoids my gaze. I'm guessing she didn't sleep at all. She's probably working because there's nothing to clean. The phone is on the table. I panic. 'You've not told Uncle Duncan, have you?' The last thing I want is him here, he'll get all militant and intrusive.

'No. I wanted to talk to you first.'

'Well, I don't want to tell him.' He'll make it into some sort of competition about what a crap father my dad is, how he's a bully, and I'll

9

have to punch him.

I grab a glass out of the cabinet and pour myself some orange juice. Linden starts to stir the batter, the dry bits assimilating as small lumps. She notices the waffle iron, which looks better since I washed it yesterday, though there's nothing I can do about the cord, which looks downright dangerous.

'How about waffles? I've not had those for years.'

I pick up the plug and the frayed cord sags. 'I don't think so.'

She stops stirring. The spoon sticks straight up in the thick goo. She puts the bowl, goop and all, in the sink. 'How about brunch at OHOP?'

'Great. I'll help you dig out your car.'

And when she kisses me lightly on the forehead, before she stomps her feet into her boots, it's not like a sister or a mother, it's like a guardian angel.

I'm on my feet too, sliding on my duck boots.

'Didn't those go out of style in the '80s?'

'Aren't those Uggs so five years ago?'

It's too cold to do the job properly and there's a thick layer of ice on the ground, beneath the snow. I use an old metal shovel, with a wooden handle that used to be red and you can still see old flecks of paint near the edges, on the underside where it's not worn as much. But basically it's worn right down to cheap pine and the metal edges are rusty with salt. When this shovel scrapes against the cement of the drive it sounds like you're working hard. Misleadingly hard. My favorite snow is wet and heavy, almost melting from the ground up and it makes pock marks when you toss it to the side into pristine snowfall. Today it's a crisp powdery snow that's fallen on a layer of ice that won't budge. I try chipping at it, but I just bend the edge of the shovel. It's been bent before and I know that soon we'll have to buy a different shovel because this one is dented into a crooked smile.

'Leave it,' Linden says. 'We'll salt it down when we're done.'

We work at a steady pace. There's a clear blue sky and my cheeks are red with the bite of the chill and exercise. I'm sweating like mad under my coat.

At the Original House of Pancakes, we're late enough to miss the churchgoers' line that often snakes its way out the door on a Sunday and we walk right in. The wood, the stained glass. Straight out of the movies. Like IHOP, only classier. *Ordinary People* was filmed here. Teenage angst, and Robert Redford directed it. There's a photo of him when you first walk in. Linden and I split a Dutch apple pancake. I get a side of bacon. We drink more coffee.

It doesn't make me jittery. Just awake. I've never been this awake before.

Outside, after brunch, Linden breathes on her key and it turns, but the doors to her car stick, frozen.

'Slam it with your hip and jiggle the handle. I've got de-icer in the trunk.' She tries to lift the trunk, it's a non-starter.

'Good plan, genius.'

She just about stops herself from giving me a quick finger, but doesn't, and up and down it pops in my direction.

But I bash my hip against the handle anyway, and it opens with a bit of effort. I push her door open from the inside with my feet.

'Nice,' she says when she sees my sole prints in salt on the inside of her door. She rubs at the marks with the elbow of her coat and puts the heat up high. It blows cold at first and I close my eyes against the force of the air. Wrap my arms around myself. Linden doesn't seem to feel this cold that's entered my bones like a slap. 'Okay kiddo, what next?'

'I've got a map project to do. Jess is coming over to work on it.'

Her eyebrows, randomly and half-heartedly plucked, lift and then settle. Her right index finger taps on the wheel. She's busy. Always busy.

'I've not had kids for a reason.' I remember hearing Linden tell a pal on the phone one time, when I'm over at hers watching the baseball.

I let her off the hook.

'Go do what you have to do. I'm sure dad will be at home when we get back. It's no big deal.'

Both of us believe this, and somehow know it not to be true. She backs out of the space, takes a left onto Greenbay. Goes slow even though the roads have been plowed and salted. At Sycamore she turns right. If we'd taken a left, we'd have hit Ridge Road.

Ages ago, feels like forever, me and my dad are riding our bikes up to Ridge Road. We're out of breath, hot because it's the height of summer, and we turn around, looking at the slope we've just struggled up.

'This used to be a beach,' he says.

I look out. It's miles and miles from the water. I can't even see the lake when we stand where the ridge flattens. He says it was a long time ago, after the glaciers melted and then it receded.

'Receded?'

'Moved back to where it is now.'

'When was that?'

Elizabeth Reeder

'Before the Indians.'

At seven I already know all about this. When the Indians lived here the lake was close to where it is now, down by our house, and they tamed young trees with strong leather straps and pointed them towards the lake so people knew where it was. Indian Trail Trees. When we walk by the trees he lets me touch the ones on the parkways. They're hundreds of years old. With elbows pointing to water, the rest of the tree growing straight and true, and I wonder how they do that.

'It's what they're born to do,' my dad says, 'grow from the earth to the sky.'

'Not point at water?'

'No, they're forced to do that.'

'Like me with my chores.'

'Exactly.'

With a light touch on the pedals, we coast most of the way home; to us that low arch of land is a climb and the reverse, the glide down, freedom. By the time we get to the trees our legs are working hard again on the flat road.

Aunt Linden always talks with special fondness about two particular Trail Trees, just a stone's throw from each other, which stand at opposite sides of a crossroads: one strong inside a fence, the other only a tall stump.

'They're like lovers looking at the sunrise,' she says every single time we drive by. Every time. Today is no different as I sit in the passenger seat, heat blasting, my stomach full up from the apple pancake and strips of crispy bacon, and she tells me the story of the blizzard of '79 and how the wind whipped, and how snow stung her face, and her fingertips burned with cold. And how her high school sweetheart kissed her, for the first time, there. She points to the middle of the road.

'What was his name?'

'It doesn't matter,' she says, 'his lips were cold and chapped. We were standing where Sycamore meets Evergreen, standing right in the middle of the road. There were no cars, the snow was deep and blowing, like the pictures you see of snow racing across the tundra.'

'Tundra?' I used to ask. But not now. I know what it is.

She pauses in her story, getting the feeling of the day back. 'We stood with our legs wide, bracing against the gales, and we held each other's arms so we could stay standing and the wind was whipping, whipping so hard, and this family appeared out of the snow, a mom and dad with a spindly rope of four young kids between them. They'd just seen *The King and I* downtown, with Yul Brynner and everything. There was some whistling going on; that's how we heard them first. This eerie whistling. You know, between the gusts, in that silence before the wind picks up again. Whistling right there. The snow was up to our thighs when we turned off the main street and there's no way the kids could have walked without help. Their parents looked exhausted trying to hold them all together. So we each picked up a kid and carried them to their house and they fed us hot chocolate and grilled cheese and we slept on their floor and in the morning everything was compacted in snow, and bright, the white, white world and we walked home in our parkas and borrowed hats. We dated for a while. The perfect beginning. The next fall he left for college.'

I think, they had sex in that family's house, on a stranger's floor, with four little kids asleep upstairs. That's what she remembers so fondly. Her first screw.

She sighs and her hands move on the steering wheel as she turns onto Sheridan. We've got a bit to go before the ravines start. The ravines mark the line between land and beach and are crumbling twenty-five foot cliffs of sand, tree roots and dirt that cut down to the lake. They start a block or so before Mrs Morse's house and reach north a few miles. That's where the glaciers stopped and retreated, that's what my dad tells me: 'They gouged out the land and left detritus.'

'Detritus?'

'Like all the clothes and toys and games and books you leave lying about your room. But bigger, even dirtier. Rubble, dirt, earth, big rocks all left behind when they melted.'

'But why don't the ravines stretch south down the lake?'

'That's because the glaciers didn't reach there,' he says, making it up.

Looking back I know he's fibbing because he has a crooked smile and a glimmer in his eye as he urges me to get back on my bike and stop asking questions he doesn't know the answers to.

Linden swerves onto Walnut Street, the rear of her car sliding ever so slightly. Walnut takes us to Forsythia, where my dad's house is, my house. She pulls into the driveway but keeps the car running. 'I'll go home and get some things I need. I've also got a solo exhibition in two weeks. Lots to do for it.'

'Where?'

Elizabeth Reeder

'Down in Boys' Town. I'll be back tonight.'

'Don't worry if you get caught up with what you're doing.'

'I'll be back tonight. Either to keep you company or to kick my brother's face in.'

The house is bright with snow and light. Two mugs on the table as usual. Only they're mine and Linden's.

My dad's out there and he's coming home. His gangly walk will bring him back. And his grin that takes his cheeks from skinny and rough to full, the smile that takes over his face, it'll be back too.

Quiz arrives at my door with a snowball in hand. Within ten minutes of me phoning him. He's nothing if not eager, my boy. My Quiz. I take a step back and he chucks the iceball at me anyway. I duck and it hits a wall. The floor white with it. I turn in mock shock. And then he's right here, bulky arms, gloved hands which he shoves up my back. Freezing. Solid. Lifting me. I ignore the cold and wrap my arms and legs around him. Plastering him with kisses. His red cold face. My hot lips. His grin. He turns and closes the door with one hand, the other firmly under my butt.

'Mr Davis?' he shouts, tentatively. Redundantly.

'He's not home.' I lean back and start to unzip his coat. Slip my hand against the solidness of his chest. Kiss his neck. Bite it just a bit. He lets go and I land on the floor.

He cleans up the mess he's made by sweeping up the broken snow in his hands. He is voluminous. He scoops and swings, wet snow flicking off in all directions. He chucks the bulk of it into the sink. Icy batter splatters up to the splashback.

'That's just gross.'

'Would-be pancakes,' I say.

And then he comes at me, his clown grin, an upturned pot for a hat, splayed jazz hands and shifting shoulders. The can-can.

He's here. Right in close. Stirring up air with his wild, flailing body. I've never laughed so hard in my life.

'No, no not again,' I say, putting my hands out in front of me.

But he does it again. His clown grin.

The tears roll down my face, my stomach aches. I don't feel hysterical, and then for a split second I do. It packs a punch to my gut. And for a flash my tears are something else, but he pirouettes with vigor, cracks his knee on the table and falls to the floor.

We're laughing, I'm crying too and we're kissing.

There's a bit of teeth to his kiss on my neck. Clumsiness, it's sweet. I breathe and it's him and me and everything all at once. Close and yet it's easy to breathe here. And I know that later I'll cry those deep, hollow tears, full of fear, that I can feel waiting for me, but for now all I want is him and me and the place where laughter and awkwardness and grace and tears leave no room for anything else.

I'm the one who asks Quiz to go. I do it nicely.

'I've got work to do,' I say. 'You better get dressed, Jess will be here any minute.'

I grin and toss him his shirt. My body is stiffer, already independent again, my smile tight at the edges. I tilt my head so my hair hides the mess of emotions in my face.

'My mom wants me home early anyway,' Quiz says. Not one to be kicked out after finally getting what he's wanted for months. It's enough that I go soft in his arms, just for a minute at the door.

'Can we do this again, sometime?' I ask.

And Quiz is luminous again. 'Anytime, Roe.'

I'm shutting down. The sun low in the sky, the sunlight long and weak.

'Bring your books and the vodka,' I say to Jess when I phone her.

My dad won't let me drink. Ever.

'It's just a few beers,' I always protest. 'You used to drink all the time in high school.'

'How do you know that?'

'Uncle Duncan told me. You'd drink under the bleachers, when you skipped classes.'

'What does he know?'

Total sidestep of the truth. Noted.

'You're being stupid, Roe. This is your life. You should be smarter with it.'

'Just a few beers,' I repeat. 'You're the one who's being stupid.'

'No, I'm being a dad.'

'Illuminate me on the difference.'

'Us dads, we're only selectively stupid.'

And this is why I can never stay mad at him for long.

Jess tells me about kissing Kevin last night at Lucy Rigg's party. She kissed him right in front of his girl.

'His girlfriend,' I correct. She rolls her eyes, nods her head.

'More vodka,' she directs, as she shoves her glass towards me and I reach for the bottle. 'More vodka for you?' she encourages, clinking my empty glass with her full one.

'No thanks.' I've only had one vodka and orange juice and it's enough. I find that now that I've got a buzz, I don't want to be lost.

'Hey, what planet are you on?' she asks.

Planet 'my dad's disappeared', I think. 'Planet Vodka,' I say.

'Lightweight.'

Five o'clock and Jess is floppy and hilarious. Even drunk she's drawing the Baltic states with true precision in her notebook; she'll ace history, like always. She amazes me. My maps suck. I can't seem to hold the names, much less their shapes in my head. And this color planning doesn't make sense, and I keep ending up with red countries smooshed together. The countries morph and change names and regimes. I have this hard feeling that I'm going to flunk this class. My head hurts. Flunking is simply not something I do.

'You can't see their borders if you do it like that. I'd use more blue and yellow, white even,' Jess suggests.

'And you think I don't know that?'

I close the stupid book and throw it over the side of the bed. It slaps the floor. I'd say that history is for losers but Jess is a total fanatic.

She continues to work on her maps and then I fiddle with math until that does my head in too: geometry, more shapes. She's still drawing, while I tackle my chemistry. And I love it. The equations. There's a logic to it that's irresistible.

She punches me on the arm. 'Pay me some attention.'

'As if. I heard you phone him when you went to the bathroom.'

'I'm shameless.' She grins, proud of the fact. 'She was there too. I could tell from the way he talked.'

Jess is incredible. The outrageousness of her flirting with a boy when his girlfriend is at his side.

'She's got brothers you know,' I remind her.

But Jess isn't afraid of anyone or their brothers. 'Whatshisface was asking for you.'

'Let him ask away,' I challenge her and manage, I think, not to blush. She'd be relentless if she knew about what Quiz and I were doing just before she arrived. Like I've sealed some loser fate by dating a rugby player.

It doesn't matter. It's six and she's got to go.

'I promised my mom. Home to play happy family.'

'See you tomorrow.'

She slides out the door and over the road and through at least three neighbors' gardens in a short cut back to her house. Over the years we've worn a path. We have to jump the fences between yards, sometimes over and back again, to avoid rose bushes, but it's faster than by road.

Night slants into the house but the light inside is soft. Today is already different than yesterday. This is not my burden alone. Tonight Linden will come back and she'll know what to do. We'll decide what to do together.

I don't know what makes it so easy for my mom to hand me over to him that day in his shop. He must seem like a nice man, this young man who has made her a set of keys. Maybe he looks familiar, maybe he has a face you can trust. I'm a newborn in her arms and I just cry and cry and cry.

He puts the keys on the counter and goes to the back of the shop, washes his hands and comes back with a bit of sweet butter on the tip of his pinky. As I suckle his finger, she notices how taken he is with me. I imagine his breath smells of coffee and his hands of metal. I stop kicking and crying.

'Where's the Ladies' room?'

He points to the small mirrorless room in the back. 'Will you hold her?' she asks and he tucks me, her baby, into the crook of one arm and says sure, like he's tipped a hat to her. An imaginary cowboy hat. And maybe she thinks that with someone like him, it'll all be okay.

'What's her name?' he asks when she comes back, his big hand clasping my infant fist.

'Roe,' she says. 'Like a deer. It's those long skinny legs.'

Hooves as hard as hammers, she doesn't say.

'Well, isn't she the sweetest thing. Bet she's a handful.'

'Not a stitch of trouble. I know she's got a tough look, but it's all for show. She'll melt the hardest heart.'

This is how I imagine my mother. The day she runs into my dad in the shop. How, even though she gets the keys she needs, she goes home with him. A man she's met only once before.

'Maybe twice,' dad says, when he tells the story.

'Where did you meet?' I ask.

'We could never decide. Maybe Albuquerque, maybe Taos.'

And I imagine how, ten days later, she quietly and neatly unclicks the four handmade bolt locks of his front door, that only keep things from the outside from getting in, and she never comes back.

You can tell by the way he tells the story that he's not interested in her. It's me he sees. 'I could see your legs kicking through the blankets,' my dad says every time he tells me this story. 'It was love at first sight.'

'I knew so little about her, about where you were from,' my Aunt Linden tells me one summer when we're watching a Cubs game at her apartment. 'I kept expecting Peter to phone in the middle of the night saying that some guy had kicked in the door, yelling that he was your real father and that he'd punched Peter out cold and taken you.'

'Not with the locks dad has on it.'

She slaps the table with her open hand. Leans in towards the TV.

'Where's the strike zone, blind man? Need some glasses?' She's yelling at the homeplate ump as our pitcher, our hot-headed pitcher, with three bad calls in this inning, bases loaded behind him, is visited by the pitching coach and taken out of the game. On his way to the dugout he swerves.

'Don't do it,' I say, leaning in, my shoulder square with Linden's. The boos and wolf calls of Wrigley Field coming in through her open windows.

But he does, he punches his face right into the umpire's. The ump whips off his mask. Our pitcher holds up one finger, then another and then another. Shakes them. Three bum calls waved before the ump. Then he's back to two fingers and then he's left with one. And he slides his middle finger right up close to the ump's face.

'Keep your head on! The idiot.'

Unceremoniously ejected.

'He's put us right in it.'

'It's his passion that makes him good.'

'And a pain in the ass.'

And this is a pain in my ass.

While the sloppy-joe defrosts over a low heat in the skillet, I search for the keys to Mrs Morse's house. They've got to be here. Although I never use them, never have reason to, dad usually hangs them by the back door so he can check for leaks and wear 'n tear.

But they're not there. His shop keys are here, and the garage key to the outside door we never use, and my keys. That's it.

His workbench is big. The size of two tables shoved together, because that's what it is. Big wooden slabs on supports. Hefty oak file drawers act as legs on each end, and in the middle. The machines of his trade are mounted to the tops, in easy reach. Above the tables, shelves run all along the wall. Pristine handmade locks in all the drawers, and antique locks sprawled, stacked and thrown on the shelves.

He keeps his work surfaces clear and clean. Like his tools. His machines. The rest of the space holy chaos, like the house. But his things, his tools of the trade, immaculate. That's him all over: completely anal, except when he's a total slob.

I pull open the first drawer and start to look for Mrs Morse's keys. If I know my dad, they'll be on a ring with a few others to other doors I don't know about. Inside the drawer it's all metal and sawdust and age. I take keys out one ring or key at a time, and put them in a pile on top when I've discounted them.

And this is what I'm doing when I hear Linden's car in the drive. I've got a few possibilities. I slide them into my pocket and push the rest back into the open drawer, only three more drawers to go. I wash my hands in the sink and give the big frozen chunk of sloppy-joe a stab, it breaks into two ground beef icebergs.

She comes in, her jeans hang low on her hips. They're workman's trousers with good pockets and a ring of denim perfect for hanging a hammer. Her head looks smaller, stuck on a thin neck. Her cheeks are pale, her dark eyes tired.

My dad or work?

'Smells great,' she says, lifting the lid of the skillet. She gives the lot a figure-eight stir.

'It needs to cook in a bit more.'

She puts the lid on again. 'Thanks for making dinner. Sorry I'm so late.'

I pick up my book and walk to the couch, she follows. She pulls her thumb on the denim hammer hook and plops down beside me. I cram my book down the side of the cushion.

Her hands are calloused, the dryness pulling her fingerprints, the cracks and rivers of lines on the palms of her hands, into tough white ridges. I go get lotion from by the sink and then I take her right hand in mine. Massage her hand a bit.

'That feels good.'

'Your hands, look at your hands.'

'I know, Roe. They're impossible to look after. How was your day?'

'Fine.' I had sex, I drank some vodka. A stellar day. 'What did you do?'

'We erected the walls at the Phoenix Gallery, did the first coat of paint. They'll have to do the rest themselves tomorrow. I have to teach.'

'What time?'

'All day.'

'What about your solo show?'

She inhales, looks out the window. Smoothes her crazy eyebrow.

'Give me your other hand,' I say. She takes it away from her brow, stretches it out to me, palm up.

'Didn't get to it. But that's fine. I'll find the time later.'

Her voice is high.

'How's your show going?'

'You know me, all smoke and mirrors until the night, but I've got eleven days and most of the images are final, printed. Some of it's at the framers. I need to…' She stops. 'I've got plenty of time.'

I take the hint, change the subject.

'I salted the driveway. We forgot to do it earlier.'

'I wish I could take you home with me.'

And there it is. So many facts at once. This isn't her home. She's not at home. And within that statement there's the fact that that's exactly what she might have to do soon if my bum of a dad doesn't drag his lazy ass through that door—sooner rather than later. Please.

'I snore and my room's a pit. Don't ask for things that might torture you later.'

'You're easy. Remember, I've lived with Peter too.'

And even though he's missing, even though my heart is ripped apart and my head aches with all this thinking and worry, I know she's right. The place is much more orderly without him.

Something falls down in the other room. We both jump to our feet. Dad's old horseshoe lies face up on the floor, it reads 'BF, New Mexico'.

Dad has it hanging like a U so that the luck doesn't run out. There are small holes in the plaster where it's pulled the two nails out of the wall.

'Looks like Mrs Morse's place isn't the only one needing some repairs.'

'Too right.'

Mrs Morse's house has a bad reputation, but we aren't far behind. Our houses both face west, backs to the lake, next door to each other but slightly staggered: her house just that bit closer to the edge of the ravine and to Lake Michigan's seasonal shifts.

Ages ago my dad knocked out one wall of our living room and replaced it with a huge stretch of triple reinforced glass so we could always see the lake. This huge space. Because of the steep cut of the ravines, we can't see the beach but we can see further out into the water, to the horizon. Even on clear days, the opposite shore of the lake over in Michigan is just too far away to spot.

Inside our house is a sparse, masculine order. Already I see the femaleness Linden leaves behind, lipstick on mugs, her perfume and bottles of shampoo and lotion in the bathroom. If you think about dust in a way that doesn't put it in the same category as dirt and germs, then me and my dad keep a clean house: floors vacuumed once a week, all kitchen counters cleaned every day. Same with the kitchen table and the bathroom.

The odd keys and locks my dad collects litter the place and I find the keys more or less like he'd pulled them out of his sleeves, a magician with an endless scarf.

The locks are a bit more bulky. Without their native environments: doors, boxes, gates, they lean at odd angles, uneasily pitched against each other on his shelves like outsized books.

I'm young, three or four years old, and dad gives me the task of picking the locks on the boxes he makes. It takes me months to learn how to open any of them. It's usually faster to find the right key among my dad's stockpile. Before I become good at picking locks, I become very good at matching keys to locks. Original, ancient keys are easier because their surfaces scar, the movement of opening and locking, locking and opening, leaves specific marks. Copies, especially bland modern keys, are nearly impossible to match up.

The locks he makes always have their own style, their own sound. Metal on metal but smooth mechanisms that end in a satisfying click. The house is full of them, even on items that don't need them: the bathroom medicine cabinet mounted to the left of the sink, made from reclaimed lake-wood, its key hanging from twine, like a dug-up pirate's chest stuck on the wall. There are Russian-doll-style music boxes, jewelry boxes, toy boxes, and an old-fashioned hope chest that sits at the end of my dad's bed. Now he leaves all these boxes unlocked, each matching key stuck on the side with twine, or masking tape, or popped inside, and then there are plain ol' locks, made for gates and doors and windows and just made, as far as I can tell, for the hell of it.

Linden is grinning. Has a bit of sauce on her cheek. Takes a slug of a beer. 'This is delicious. Mom never cooked the onions all the way through.'

'That's what dad always says. Grandma was the lowest common denominator, he could only do better.'

'Meow. Who says girls are the catty ones?' Linden takes another big bite of bun and sloppy-joe, she's halfway through chewing when she adds a few potato chips to the mix. 'His barbecue is the best though. He always impresses people with it.'

'Like who?'

'The guys he worked with when he was out west.'

'He doesn't talk about that much.'

'I'm not surprised. His lost years.'

'Lost?'

She takes another bite, looks at me over the top of her bun. Raises an eyebrow. But doesn't grin. And I know I'm not going to find out exactly how he was lost. Drugs, drink, sex, disoriented in the desert, a vision-quest? What?

'I went out to visit him once and he was living on some ranch in New Mexico, building a fence as part of some artist's 'bigger canvas', and after that he met and hung out with some random weirdo artist in Arizona and helped him to put together some sort of environment sculpture in some woebegone place.'

'Woebegone?'

'Bumble-fuck.'

BF. Ah, the definitions change all the time.

'I gave him the horseshoe.'

'I didn't know that.'

'Bet he didn't tell you what BF meant either.'

'He's old-fashioned that way.'

'God. He was skinny as poles back then. Beautiful to watch. I shouldn't say that since I'm his sister, but it's true. The beard, his long sun-bleached hair, his disappearing ass.'

We laugh. Not much changed then.

'He wore jeans like they were originally meant to be worn, more dust than denim holding them together. His cowboy boots and hat.'

'Spurs and all?'

'Nah. No horses. Can you imagine?'

'It wouldn't be pretty.'

'The artist he was helping looked all east coast, but there were two or three other laborers who looked just like Peter.'

She drifts back, sighs. I wonder how many of the cowboys she slept with.

'They lived in a cabin they'd built at the beginning of the project. Just planks of wood but those boys kept that place neat. I never understood how. It's like the desert horizon demanded it. The natural order of things had to be adhered to.'

My dad neat? Anywhere but his workbench? Can't imagine it.

'It was truly bumble. Too much. So much space. It freaked me out, but not Peter. He was in his element.'

'Why had he gone out there?'

She doesn't answer me. I can't tell if it's a swerve or if my question just threatened to break her flow.

'He was happy there. Or, if not happy, he seemed to be in the right place. The right place for him anyway.' She adds, 'At the time.'

'And when he came back?'

'He was happy here too. Wanted to be with dad. And then you showed up.' She traces her jaw. Then mine. Her fingers are rough as sandpaper. 'He has,' she says, 'a way of always being content where he is, right up to the point where he can't bear it a moment longer.'

Not bear me a moment longer.

Linden is beside me in my bed and I'm holding myself still. Trying to make my breathing sound normal. It's hit me so hard I can't move. One second I'm fine, the next I can't breathe. I try to stay calm and steady. I fail miserably. I'm on my back and the tears flow down either side of my head, pool in my ears, wet my pillow. I am quiet at first. Linden's breath steadies into sleep. I

Elizabeth Reeder

let out a gulp. Her hand seeks out mine. She squeezes. I turn away.

'It's okay Roe.'

I just can't. Can't rely on her. Have her see me like this. She reaches to turn on the light.

'Don't.'

'Okay, honey.'

When she pulls me towards her I grieve. I let go. I give in. I am thin and long and empty.

I hate this feeling. I sit up and open a cold draft into the bed, my back is to her, my face protected by the dark, my hair. The freeze blows under the covers, through my pajamas. She puts her hand on my back. Slow soft circles.

'Shhh,' she says.

I wipe my face with my hands. Salt on my tongue. Crusty bits on the inside of my eyes.

'I'm getting up.'

'Me too.'

'No.' I find my slippers and a robe and close the door behind me.

I start with the second drawer of keys and make it through them all before exhaustion takes hold. I've got loads of possibilities. I put all the rest of the keys back in the correct drawers as I go. I stuff the keys down the side of the couch, curl up and sleep there, and you can't tell I've been in my dad's things at all.

MONDAY

'I tried to wake you,' Linden's note reads in the morning. 'I've got an early class, but I'll pick you up from school.'

The rug just inside the door is wet, like she's gone out and come back and the snow-shake off her boots has melted. She's been down to the lake. The new snow, the wind, the rough water. All of it icy and unhelpful.

There's a pot of coffee waiting for me.

'P.S. Don't forget to eat something.'

Food is the last thing I want. But I know she's right. It's what you do in the morning. I make two BLTs. I slide one into my school bag for lunch and take the other one with coffee to the living room so I can watch the lake. The bread sticks to the roof of my mouth, the coffee helps, its bitterness is just right.

In chemistry I'm stuck with spotty Scott. He sits too close. Food in his teeth. Breath rank with breakfast and dinner and plaque. Big spots, pus-heads. He's ugly and that's gross, but the problem is he's dumb. With a capital D. Dumb.

I try not to talk with him at all. I'm aware that last year he evacuated the building with his mistake in biology. I can't even comprehend what you could do with a dead frog that would cause mass hysteria. He managed it. He's a mistake of biology.

His stiff fingers crowd the test tubes. His grin has a bit of bread in it.

I try not to breathe in but I do try to stop him from pouring the contents of one tube into the other. When I don't succeed, I'm the first one to the door.

There are no flames but plenty of smoke and fumes and the main alarm goes off. Four fire engines arrive. We're out back on the track field. Freezing. There's got to be some law against this. But it's not a drill. It's the real thing. A few kids nip down to smoke some cigarettes by the train station or swig from hipflasks behind the goal posts. The explosion has flushed Jess out of gym and she's standing by the corner of the building with her hips pushed right up close to Kevin. I don't see his girlfriend but I know exactly where this is headed. Jess is always the other girl. It's almost like she seeks it out. Like it's a requirement. 'Boyfriend wanted, must have sexy car and blonde girlfriend. Catastrophic break-up imminent.'

I scan and find Quiz, he's standing with some rugby buddies.

'Hey, Roe.' He's non-committal.

'Hey, Quiz.' I give a single sway to my hips, raise my hand towards his pals. 'John. Chris.'

'Hiya, Roe.'

Quiz reaches out his hand. I take it. He rubs my arm with the other. 'See you later guys,' he says. And we walk out towards the far side of the field.

'It was my lab partner who did this.'

'No kidding?'

'I couldn't stop him. He guarded the phials with his zits and laughed this hideous, maniacal laugh.'

'Well, you got me out of Math. So I thank you.'

The bells ring, on and off, and we have to go back in. We can't go back to the lab, it's still a bit too toxic. They herd us would-be chemists into the auditorium and we get an ad hoc and non-specific talk about safety. About one partner looking out for the other. I shove a finger up and down first towards spotty Scott and then towards Ms Clunes who really should know better than to chastise her strongest student in front of the whole class for the quite reasonable action of not putting herself between her psycho lab partner and his death wish.

'Okay kids.'

We all hate it when he calls us that. Today Mr R pauses, looks at us. I wonder what he sees. He's looking like he's been dragged through shrubs backwards.

'Today, we're going to talk about…' He licks his lips, runs his hands through his hair, when his fingers get jammed a bit, he pushes on through. Second time they run smooth. 'I've been thinking about space. About how every space, every place, has its natural order. Where the molecules are in their natural state. Every time you or I move in space, we displace the natural order. Every time you move, you stir things up.'

Mr R has a theory for everything, it's not really a Communications class, it's a make-it-up-by-the-seat-of-your-pants philosophy class.

'What about light? Does that change the natural state?' Overenthusiastic Freddie doesn't raise his hand, just jumps in. Today Mr R doesn't mind. We're witnessing a new world order.

'Good question.' He pauses, his eyes steady on us all, yet flicking, absent between words. 'Let's say a room is dark. A light slices across. What is displaced?'

Silence.

'Has anything physically changed?'

'Yes. The whole room is transformed.' Freddie again.

'But physically altered?'

Sandy, the science geek, 'Yes, light is energy.'

'Sure,' says Mr R, 'yes and no. It passes through but does not take up any room. Any space. It simply affects the molecules that are already there.'

'But it alters our perceptions.'

'Exactly.'

'What if it heats them up?' Sandy again.

'Well, then I suppose that's a bit different. The same molecules get excited, then calm down. But once the light, the heat, is gone, they remain the same as they were before.'

Place. Space. Displacement.

So I'm sitting there thinking that everything we do is bound to upset this world. To throw out of whack what is perfect without us. What a load of crap. Natural order has to be active, to account for all the life about us.

'Aren't presence and movement part of order, a living order?' I suggest.

'In an ideal world, Roe, that might be the case. The truth of the matter is that absence is presence. That's the reality of it. It restores what has been upset and disrupted. What has become disrupted. Sometimes for years.'

'So if we all left right now,' smart-alec James, 'then it'd be okay because it'd be the way things are supposed to be?'

Mr R looks out the window, at an unpeopled expanse of mazed sidewalks and frozen grass, his hand plays at the muscles of his jaw and then follows the bone and then the red-brown wiry hair to the end of his lumberjack beard. He twirls some beard-hair between his index finger and thumb. His eyes, well, they're not here anyway.

We're all silent. I've never seen an adult come apart before. But this is it. His actions are empty and watery.

'You know people who never just stay in one place? Those people who never try to work it out but they just flee? Well, it's better that they go. It replaces the natural order.'

I look at his left hand, an indentation at the base of his ring finger. The ring gone, he's had his natural state reinstated.

It's just like with keys. Lock and key and how we think they make things whole when they come together, but what if it's just the opposite, the lock is whole, a complete entity on its own and the key invades, pushes the molecules into unnatural spaces, tumbler and pin, and turns it.

But what if the natural order is with the two of you there? Right there. And when one goes, the air invades, displaces and everything is off kilter, unnatural. Space as the invading presence? As the opposite of the state of grace?

'Hmmm,' starts sweet-faced, but tricky as a fox, Missy McLaughlin who leads the field hockey team to victory after victory with her underhand tactics, 'what does this have to do with communication?'

'It's about its breakdown,' Mr R says.

And before the bell, which is just sound and not presence, invades this space, and before this opportunity reverts to the reality of a normal class, all twenty-two of us slide out of our chairs and into the perfectly balanced, waiting hall.

My locker is a mess. My jeans are too tight, my hair just looks like shit. My locker has one pile of papers and hard folders leaning to the left, on top of that another leans to the right and then my running gear is crammed in the mini-compartment up top, my shoes bending unnaturally every time I have to shove the door closed. I lean my head against the chaos. The bell rings and the world is loud behind me. Everyone moving. I can't get my feet to go. Who cares?

I spend lunch in an empty classroom and then it's onto history. My maps suck and at the end of another class full of dates and mind-numbing facts, Mr Pavich hands out the tests we took on Friday. Every test but mine. The bell rings. 'Miss Davis, will you stay after class please? The rest of you can go.'

Jess elbows me on her way out, her A+ test smug in her hands. 'Uh-oh.'

'Up to my desk,' he says, pointing a finger at me and then crumpling it in towards his nasty little chin.

'You can't seem to see the boundaries, Roe. It's a real problem.' He pauses, for the drama of the moment. 'It's easy, these countries are one thing and then they're another. They can't be more than one thing at a time.'

That's me all over. A problem with borders, with boundaries.

'You can't just make it up,' he continues, small pinched face, greasy grey hair, linear pea-brain.

Why? Why can't I? This isn't history. It's making silly lines on a piece of paper. Where's anything that matters? Where are the people? The passions? Where's the history?

He turns the test over, slowly, like a flag unfurling.

F minus. In red. Nearly covers the whole page.

His mean beady eyes on me, creepy, full of misplaced power: I'm not just bad at this, I'm atrocious; I don't even belong on the academic scale. It's on the table between us. He's relishing it. Stating the obvious.

F minus.

A made-up grade for a girl who makes things up.

'You'll need to have your parents sign this, to prove to me they know exactly what you're up to.'

'I don't have a mom.'

But this doesn't faze Pavich. He doesn't want to hear it. Doesn't matter. Countries go to war, entire towns wiped out. A line moves. What do my petty problems matter? These maps are important. I should prioritize.

I want to say, my dad's missing. I can't get you the signature you want. I want it to matter, make a difference. But it doesn't. Things explode, wives leave, teachers go off the rails, dads abandon their posts.

The former Yugoslavia, the former USSR, the former me.

'Sure thing.'

'You better study extra hard for the test on Wednesday.'

'Harder than I've ever studied for anything in my life. From this point on my life is empty of everything but lines on a map.'

'Glad to hear it.'

As I leave the room, I feel him watching my ass, the Nazi, fascist perv. Outside the door, Jess leans with her back against the row of lockers. Her legs are crossed casually at the ankles, her stomach bare. I flip the test paper out towards her.

'No way.'

'Yes, way.'

'I didn't know you could get a F minus.'

'You can't, Jess. He's just making a point. The creep.'

'He's not that bad.'

'Your talent blinds you to the facts.'

'You want to ditch ninth period and go to Carl's?'

'Can't. Linden's picking me up and we're going shopping.'

'Is she still staying at your house?'

'Yup. Her pipes burst. She needed a place to stay until they're fixed. Can't get a plumber until Thursday.'

Dad will be back by then.

'Call me later.'

'Of course. What are you going to do?'

'Nothing.'

And I know this nothing is called Kevin.

Linden has tried to clean herself up. I know that. Beneath her parka, which she opens as soon as we're inside the police station, she's got on black baggy trousers, a push-up bra, a small sweater and the ends of the shirt hang down below it. Her hair smells of smoke when I hug her. And her fingers are a mess. Black underneath the nails. I hold one hand, turn it palm up and then back again.

'I forgot my nail brush, sweetie. Surely it won't matter.'

As soon as we enter, Quiz's mom, Officer Berg, crosses the room towards us and I know the chain of events to come. She looks stiffer in full police uniform, a lump of panic sticks in my throat. Linden has no idea who she is.

'We'd like to file a missing person's report,' Linden says.

'Who's gone?'

'My brother, her dad.'

Mrs Berg looks at me. I smile. Inanely. How inappropriate can my responses be? 'Linden, this is Quiz's mom. Mrs Berg, this is my aunt Linden.'

'Quiz didn't mention this to me.'

Linden looks at me. Mrs Berg looks at me. 'He doesn't know,' I say.

Her tone softens and she becomes more business-like and yet more like a mom, more like the woman I've met a few times before, usually in the Berg kitchen. She directs her questions at me, which I'm grateful for. 'Since when?'

'Since Friday night.'

'Who saw him last?'

'Me.'

'What time?'

'Around midnight. He kissed me goodnight.'

'Anything strange about that night? Or the week before? Has he seemed under stress or done anything out of character?'

My chest is clasped hands.

I raise my eyes slowly. 'I didn't notice anything.'

I will not cry. I will not cry. Linden weaves her hand through mine. Lock and key.

My dad knows how to make the spaces within locks fit into any shape, he can change the shape at will. My hands slot into his perfectly any time. *Berwyn. Doors open on the left at Berwyn.* Which state is the natural, the right state?

'Did he leave a note?'

'Nope.'

'What did he take with him?'

'Boots. A big coat, a hat. His wallet. His lockpicking equipment, I think. Some keys.'

Mrs Berg leans over in confidence, smiles. 'I locked myself out of the car once, and was late for my after-school run. On his way to help me, he picked Quiz up from school. He's good at what he does,' she says.

'He often goes out after dark and practices picking these difficult old locks he keeps just for this reason. He practices opening them without light. He says it keeps him sharp.'

Mrs Berg smiles, but it's a short one. Then she turns to Linden. Sharply. Both hands flat on the counter, all business.

'Is this the first time he's done something like this?'

'Of course it is.' I say.

Linden shifts. Unfolds her hand from mine. Looks at me and then at Mrs Berg.

'No, it isn't. He's done this before,' says Linden. I see the side of her face, it's crumpled up.

'What?' My voice is shrill. Loud. 'What are you talking about, he's never, he's always been right here. This isn't like him, not at all.'

Linden steps in closer, all her attention on me. I bat her hand away.

'Roe, honey. He used to. In his teens and twenties. I've not known how to tell you.'

'What? But I've never… That doesn't matter. It doesn't mean anything. He's not done a thing like this since he had me.'

'That's not exactly true.'

My lips are a hard line. My arms cross.

'When you were small, a toddler, he brought you over to my apartment. Middle of the night, with an overnight bag, diapers. I mean, you were still small, a baby. He handed you to me, and put the keys to his house on my hall table, in case I needed anything.'

My chest isn't tight, it's a fortress.

'He said he'd be gone a day. He was gone nearly two weeks.'

I don't believe her. Can't believe her. 'My dad never did that.'

'Sweetie. I'm not saying this to hurt you.' She doesn't move any closer, but her tone is more apologetic, intimate when she continues, 'Roe, that wasn't the only time.'

I can't think. Not just one time? Other times? What other times? I blink. Look from one face to another. I'm sweating beneath my coat, my hands are stiff, a muscle running down my back is burning, throbbing.

Linden continues, 'The police need to know this, the more the police know, the better they'll be able to do their jobs. The sooner he'll be home.'

Linden's never been anything but honest to me. Her tells: when she touches her face, when she takes an extra second and breathes deep. She does neither.

'Roe, honey. Why don't you go get a soda? I'm going to talk to Linden for a while.'

'Or you can stay Roe. It's your choice.' Linden doesn't look at Mrs Berg, she looks at me. She isn't a mom. It's not her role to protect me from the facts, she knows this. 'I'm sorry Roe. I should have said earlier. I didn't know how.'

My head goes down, my hair in front of my face. Something's damaged. He's gone and we need to find him. The metal edged counter, the sound of phones, the clean lines of the uniforms, Mrs Berg's good intentions, Linden's guilt and worry. I don't want to hear anymore.

'I think I'll go to Carl's and get something to drink.'

Linden gives me no warning and has me in a hug. Light and quick so I can't react. Photo chemicals cling to her hair. I hear her rough hands on my coat. I unfold her arms from around me, hold her hands.

'You need to take care of your hands,' I say. 'They're a mess.'

'I know.' She smiles and tells me what I know she has to: 'Roe, I've had to call Duncan and Mel. They'll be at the house when we get back.'

My Uncle Duncan, the world's most anally organized oaf and his slow food gardening wife, the lovely I-had-a-lapse-in-judgment-when-I-married-him Mel.

'You sure are on a roll with the bad news.'

She laughs. 'I promise he won't be there for long.'

My buttons slide one after the other through the eyes of my coat. I pull up my collar and walk out into the cold.

Carl is bending some poor guy's ears about those damn mountain lions. His slate-grey formica counters stretch, chrome edges spit and polished with a long mirror mounted on the wall running behind the counter. He's hung pictures of wilderness above it and in the alcoves of all the booths: mountains, lions, birds of prey. Why does Carl live here? His heart is so obviously someplace else.

'The strongest beast out there,' he continues, making no move to fill an order.

'Sure. Whatever you say…' The customer, tall in a business suit, forties, well-to-do, leans in a bit to read the name sewed into his shirt, 'Carl. That'll be a bold filter, please.'

The please is forced through gritted teeth. His diamond studded watch prominent at his wrist. Tic toc.

'They've been spotted out in the Blue Ridge Mountains. They say there are no "official" sightings.' Carl's fingers bend in the air, punctuating his face. 'One of the greatest predators ever. They don't just disappear. Consummate hunters, they know when to retreat. Hunt carefully.'

Elizabeth Reeder

'Fascinating. Really Carl. Can I just have my coffee?'

'Sure thing, pal. No need to get snippy. They're grace in motion those cats. Pure athletes.'

The guy brushes past me on his way out. Knocks my shoulder a bit.

'Hey,' I say to him, lifting my hands which say *watch where you're going, Bud*.

'Hey yourself,' he says and pushes the door with his arrogant, thick-ringed fingers.

'Asshole.'

Carl smiles at me, pulls a cloth from his waistband and wipes the counter. 'How you doing today?'

'I'm doing, and you?'

'Just fine. How's Peter? I never saw him Saturday and the shop is still closed today.'

'He had a few call outs on Saturday early, forgot to leave a note for me, then it was too cold to be bothered and he came home. He's at a conference this week for a few days.'

'He usually puts up a sign.'

'Yeah. He's just busy.'

I make a mental note to go look in at the shop, put a sign up.

Carl nods sagely. 'What can I get you?'

'A coffee.'

'No mug today?'

'Can I have a loan?'

And he says yes, even though both of my previous loans became owned without any money changing hands.

'Sitting in?'

I nod. 'For a few, anyway.'

'I'll bring it over.'

The frother goes and I know he's doing it again. Hot chocolate for this girl.

'Carl, I mean it. You'll give an asshole what he asks for, but not me?'

His face is blank. Hurt. He stops doing the milk. No wonder I'm abandoned. I'm mean. And rude.

'Carl…'

'I'm just watching out for you, Roe.'

'I know.' He's a beautiful beast. Male pattern balding, lumberjack

34

shoulders, narrow waist. 'Compromise?'

'De-caf coming up.'

I slide into a booth, an eagle in flight gliding in a frame to my right. A quote below it, "An absence of evidence is not evidence of absence." Scott Weidensaul, *The Ghost With Trembling Wings*. What the hell does that mean? I call Jess.

'Hiya my long-legged friend.'

'Hi, Jess.'

'Thought you were going shopping with Linden.'

'Got bored. Ditched her. Wanna meet me at Carl's?'

'Can't.'

'Please, Jess. My day's been sucky.'

'One little F and you've gone all Jane Eyre on me?'

'F minus.'

'Whatever. He's a dickhead. It'll be fine.'

'I'm going to flunk out.'

'No, you aren't.'

'I can't flunk. My dad'll freak.'

'No biggy, Roe. You call me when that happens. I'll deal with him.'

'Whatever.'

'Or you could drop the class. You've got until Thursday.'

'How do you know that?'

'Let's just say geometry bites.'

'So, come on. I'll buy you a cap.'

'No can do. I'm busy.'

'Hi Roe!'

It's Kevin loud in my ear. As if I need his greeting to know it.

'Hi Kev!'

I sound so cheery that Carl, who's nearly at my table with my drink, takes a step back, raises a hand in protection. A hand out in peace, I take the mug.

'Can I talk to Jess again?'

'Wanna come drinking?'

'Can't Kevin. My aunt's here, gotta have dinner with her.'

'Bummer.'

'Can you put Jess back on?'

Kissing sounds. Kev and Jess sitting in a tree.

'Okay. Okay Jess. You've convinced me. You've got better things to do.'

'Not better... Okay. A bit better.'

'Bye.'

'Call me later.'

But we both know she means, if you can't get off your lazy unsociable ass, then don't bother calling until tomorrow.

As I leave I have the urge to hug Carl. To kiss his cheek. To have him hug me. To be protected.

'It's cold out there. Wrap up warm, Roe.'

'I'll bring this back ASAP.' I lift the mug.

When he gives me a short wave, his hand is big and wide and open.

Two cars in the drive. All the lights in the house on. Maliciously bright. Duncan's deep voice intrudes as soon as I open the door.

'You should have called us yesterday. Saturday even.'

I drop my bag on the floor, put my keys on the ring. Mel's put a narrow bunch of dried winter herbs on the table. Rosemary and thyme. A small bouquet.

I've got coffee in my hand, without any punch. I put it down on the counter.

Linden smiles, Mel gets up and gives me a hug. Her cheeks smell of lavender, her fingers, when she holds my face, smell like the earth and wild garlic.

Uncle Duncan is at my dad's workspace, poking and prodding, being his normal, controlling, intruding self. The air has shrunk towards him. His hands seem to own things when he touches them. And they become somehow less of my dad's. Who'd come back for stuff that wasn't yours anymore?

'Hey sweetheart. How you holding up?'

'It's no big deal.' I keep saying it. It's fine. 'He'll be back anytime.'

'That's what I've just been saying. I'm not going to start to worry until he's been gone a week.' Linden says.

Mel nods, but her eyes are non-committal. What other things don't I know about? She slides her arms loosely around my back, gently squeezing my upper arm.

Uncle Duncan panics through all my dad's things. Searching for scraps. Demanding every story I have of my dad. Details.

Tell me about Friday night.

About his insomnia.

About the keys.

About how he acted before the other times he left.

Insomnia. The keys. What other times?

He runs his hands over dad's workspace. I am immediately, rudely, on edge. All his questions, all his prying.

Mel's hand slices the air in front of her neck, her voice a scythe. 'Duncan, cool it.'

Oil onto a fire.

Uncle Duncan holds up a box. It's my favorite. Cut around the knot in the wood, one side curves out and back again into a square. And I already know what it contains. Nothing. 'What a ridiculous shape. What's in this one?'

'It's not my dad's,' even though it's on his worktop. 'It's mine.'

I know I sound petulant, you know, like a toddler, a terrible two. That's how I feel. It's my house. His stuff. My stuff. It's definitely not Uncle Duncan's stuff.

I grab the box and put it on the stairs to take it up later. 'There's nothing here.'

'Sure there is. Lots of clues here.'

'Nothing's changed. He didn't take anything with him,' I lie. Everything's changed. How am I supposed to know what he took with him?

'With all this mess, how can you tell?'

'I just can.'

The keys have their proper places: little hooks on the driftwood holder by the door, hung too close to the window, and a burglar could just smash the window and snatch the keys. Dad keeps loads of small, dirty keys in our kitchen drawers and I wouldn't even know where to begin to look for the things they open. Not even a clue.

There could be things missing. How the hell should I know everything he had? Uncle Duncan points to the picture hanging above dad's workspace.

'Isn't this Old Morse's?'

'Ten out of ten to the observant archivist.'

I fight the urge to bite his fingers. Kick his shins.

'Why does he have a picture of that?'

'Peter was working on making the perfect key for the lock.' Mel says.

'Why's he doing that?'

Just because. I don't know why. For Mrs Morse, I suppose. 'Just because he is.'

'That's stupid. He's never been right in the head since…'

'Don't start, Duncan.' Mel interrupts, gets up, tries to stop his hands.

He shakes her off. 'As a kid he was always over at that lady's house. I found her creepy, but he… he'd spend days, nights sometimes, over there. He used to steal things from the old witch. We should go over to her house.' Duncan makes a move for the backdoor.

I stand between him and the exit. Protecting my dad and Mrs Morse at the same time.

'We can't get in,' I say.

'What?'

'I can't find the keys to her house. He must have taken them with him.'

'Why would he do that?'

'So it'll still be here when he comes back.' I say it pointed-like but Duncan misses it. Dad spends a lot of time over there, has a headlamp and an old kerosene lantern for the purpose. The comforting orange glow coming from across the way. The headlamp and the lantern are sitting on the basement steps.

'Whatever you say.' Duncan looks out the window at Mrs Morse's house. 'Look at the state of the place. It's an eyesore. Always has been. If Peter wasn't over there, failing to stop the inevitable decline of the place, he'd be tinkering with clocks and locks and watches and anything that could be tinkered with.'

Uncle Duncan runs his eyes over all of dad's things. Picks up another box, one of the music boxes. 'Did you know that when Peter was thirteen he made a padlock and locked me in the cellar.'

Linden laughs. 'I remember that. You yelled and yelled. Remember I tried to feed you under the door. A smooshed Snickers or something.'

'How would I know? You never got it underneath.'

'I was three, Duncan.' She swallows a 'jesus'.

'Peter stood outside for ages saying that he'd lost the key. When he came home, your grandpa had to hit it with a sledgehammer.'

'What happened to dad?' I ask.

'Grandpa sent Peter to his room. Big deal. He should have been belted.'

Uncle Duncan rubs the side of his face when he talks. Pulls on his ear, like he pulls on mine. I extract pieces from his story and glue them to snatches of stories my dad tells me.

My dad says Uncle Duncan dared him to lock him in. Uncle Duncan called him a geek for wasting his time with all those locks and keys; said he couldn't keep a mosquito locked out with those rattling things. Dad always seems happy he proved Duncan wrong.

Grandpa pulled dad aside the next day, whispering 'How'd you do it?' Proud of a son who could build a lock like that. Dad says grandpa had always wanted to be good with his hands but he was, instead, an accountant, good with numbers, very good with numbers, but not so good with objects, with kids, with anything requiring co-ordination.

Dad tells me that when he moved back here, when his dad got ill, he used to let my grandpa sit in the shop as he worked and once in a while his dad would ask if he could cut a key, just a practice key, but dad wouldn't let him. His hands just weren't steady enough. Dad shakes his head and slows down in his telling, polishing the key with scant attention. 'Now old Mrs Morse, I'd trust her with any machine,' he says.

Mrs Morse hadn't always been old and despite what some people say, she was nothing like a witch at all. She was all dirt, and worn hands, and annie-get-your-gun type in-your-face practical. Maybe she got a bit batty when half her house fell into the water all those years ago. But that's what you'd expect of almost anyone in those circumstances.

'Standing in the old part of the house used to feel like you were standing on the edge of the world,' my dad says. 'The walls were so thin the wind just whistled right through.'

When he was little, my dad used to help her with the heavier chores in the garden, like lugging the wheelbarrow and pulling up weeds. Old Mrs Morse would feed my dad lemonade and tollhouse cookies. Or gigantic gingerbread men with candycorn for eyes, firecandy for mouths, and lip-buckling sour, dried cranberries for hearts. When he was a teenager and the lake waters were rising, he helped her move furniture to the new bit of the house, to the rooms furthest towards the road, away from the earth falling down the ravine. It took two of them to move her treasured door to safety.

'That door's an heirloom,' he says, and the door has pride of place: secured to the floor, frame and all; it's a working door, surrounded by the open air of her living room, opening North-South, a sliver of presence in the view out to the lake to the east. 'She put it there to remind the lake, and herself, that the water hadn't won—well, maybe one small fight, but definitely not the whole battle,' dad says. Her dad, Mr Watson, had built the house in two stages. He built one half with his bare hands, when he had just arrived in the country, and had no money, and the only thing of substance was the larger-than-life carved door his immigrant parents had brought over from Scotland.

'Looted it, most likely, if I know my da's family,' she tells me the year before she died.

'Looted?'

'Stolen. Anyone else would have taken jewelry, something they could put in their pockets,' she says, 'but not them, not a practical bone in their bodies. They stole a door and then carried it across an ocean.'

The other half of the house was built once the stock market took off and her dad had found himself with money. Real money. 'Eventually he squandered that too.'

'Squandered?'

'What you do with your allowance.'

And you could tell that he'd never invested in the older bit of the house. Even in the pictures taken before the collapse, the part of the house nearest the lake never looked like it'd last.

'You just knew it was going to go,' my dad tells me. The lake has been far back for years, with a long beach stretching from the ravine to the water's edge and it is hard to imagine waves biting into the dirt and tree roots. But the pictures prove they did. My dad always says that the lake works in a cycle with the sun or something and when the sun rages, the lake comes up and swallows some of what had been taken from it.

The remaining half of Morse's house is sturdy, but in need of repair. It has dug-down, concrete foundations, solid brickwork behind a sandstone façade which faces out towards the neighborhood, but it's in need of some paint, some work with rotted window frames and porch, missing stonework, and its roof leaks. She could have moved, got a new house, one of the condos with a lake view, but instead she lives in the ramshackle house right up until the end. Until social services forcibly moves her into an old folks home and she dies. The Village has been threatening to tear it down because they say it's a public safety hazard.

'Peter was a bully,' says Duncan.

'At school?' I ask.

'Peter didn't spend much time at school.'

'Where was he?'

'Out back under the bleachers with Steve or later with a string of girls.'

I know about the drinking. But not about the kissing.

'How'd he manage that?'

'Your guess is as good as mine.'

'They still talked about Peter when I went there.' Linden says, only she's proud of dad's reputation. 'We're talking ten years between us. "Hope your parents have learned how to raise kids since then," they'd say to me. But his problems were random. He passed his classes, was never suspended or anything like that. He was just a workshop geek who liked his tools and his grass.'

'Linden, watch what you're saying,' a flick of his eyes in my direction.

'You watch what *you're* saying. He's only been gone three days. That's nothing.'

'That's everything. He's left her,' he jerks his thumb at me. 'He's just abandoned her.'

Thanks for rubbing it in.

Mel holds up her hand, exasperated. 'Peter's just being Peter. Just the same as before. It's just what he does.'

'And it's never been okay. You two cover up for him and that's why he goes, he knows he'll get away with it. Because he always does.'

Duncan's obviously done with politeness. 'He's left Roe. Shouldn't we be angry? Shouldn't we make him come back. Make him take some responsibility?'

'Okay, Duncan. You go and do that. Go find him and drag him back.'

Linden twirls a pen round her fingers. 'He'll be back of his own accord. We can talk then.'

So much for trying to put the kid at ease. They're all hopeless. De-escalate. Distract. Distract. I see a music box, which holds smaller boxes nestled inside like Russian dolls, just sitting there where Duncan has put it down. I pick it up and grab a metal file from one of the shelves.

'What, is that something that'll help us?' asks Uncle Duncan, with an excited step forward. Annoyed that he didn't realize it first. I ignore him.

I hand Mel the box. 'Pick the lock,' I say as I slide the metal pick into her palm.

'I don't know how.'

'Just stick it in and fiddle a bit. Dad made it with an easy catch.'

'It's not really my thing.'

'I first did this one when I was four. Just try it Mel.'

Mel runs her hands over the top of the box, grasps the sides and turns the lock face up on her lap. The wood is beautiful. Cherry oak from a neighbor's tree that came down in a storm in '99. Dad cleared the street, took the wood. It's a work of art in her hand.

She tries and fails. Grimaces. 'It's really not my thing.'

'Close your eyes.'

And she fiddles. The box pops open, a voice tweaks out... 'one, two, three strikes you're out...' Harry Caray's voice rattles out, an old recording off the TV. Tinny like a music box. The big box rests on her lap, now open. She pulls out the next smallest box.

Linden laughs.

Mel looks up, beams. It's my dad all over.

'This is fabulous, Roe. Just fabulous.'

'Just fantastic.' Uncle Duncan turns to me, goes to take hold of both my arms. As if he's going to shake me. I step back, out of his reach. 'No idea where he is?' he barks.

'Absolutely no idea.'

Linden pulls Duncan back towards a chair. I touch my dad's workspace, shifting back the locks and tools which Uncle Duncan has moved. Like I'm checking for something that's missing.

'Everything's here,' I say. It's true, and, it's also absolutely a lie. He's not here.

They want to get rid of me so they can talk about adult things, things they don't want to say in front of me. Steam is coming out of the top of Duncan's head. Can't be bothered to talk to a child. But I refuse to leave the room.

Duncan starts pacing. His small, ugly eyes, his fidgeting hands. Out. I want him out.

Our occasional grandfather clock swings into life, out darts a bird. Cuckoo. And it halts again with the bird still hanging there. Boing. Boing.

I take Duncan's arm, start leading him to the door. 'We're glad you came by. Thanks for your concern.' Mel smiles, ever so slightly. There's only one way to deal with this man.

On their way out, Duncan gives me a tight, gagging hug. He smells like wet paper and dust. Mel takes my hand when she kisses my cheek, she whispers, 'Come over anytime.'

The lake is quiet outside. I reach out, play with a ring of old keys off the keyhooks. The keys are cold. Tonight Linden will sleep in my dad's bed. Clean sheets. It's fast, this movement towards a new world order. He's already gone. His space isn't his. There's no room for him.

And it's not fair.

'He used to do this sort of thing all the time. Disappear for weeks, months,' Duncan says on his way out the door. 'I never understood what he was looking for.'

'Let it rest.'

'We've got to…'

'We will,' says Mel.

'It's not like he'd disappear exactly,' continues Duncan, fully aware of the implications, 'it's just that none of us knew where he was for a little while. He usually let you know he was going, like shouting on his way out the door, "I hate all of you!" or "This is a hellhole!"'

'Or he'd leave a note,' says Linden.

'Yes, there's usually a note,' says Mel.

'He does have a temper though. Linden, remember that guy Jeremy you dated? Remember when he punched Peter? And Peter laid him flat, in response?'

'Bye, Duncan,' says Linden. 'See you soon, Mel.'

Linden stands at the window, waving, a smile plastered on her face. Their engine starts. 'My brother the asshole, the shit-stirrer.'

I take a slower look at everything. A box, a key or two that could be missing. And the folder. His folder with his notes about the key, it's green, a bit grimy because he carries it everywhere. And it's not here.

I keep picturing us at the table. All the signs I didn't see, his bag by the door, the papers sticking out of the top. They're not here anymore.

'Jeremy…' Linden pauses, 'I can't remember his last name; he was a stalk from the floor to the ceiling. He had to stoop to get through doorways. He wasn't flash or all that smooth, but tall, reedy. Yeah. A bit aggressive. Peter didn't really deserve that punch. Jeremy wasn't really my type,' she says.

Personally I can't imagine anyone who isn't her type. She's Linden, different day, different guy.

'What is your type?'

'Don't you start too.'

'I mean it.'

She looks at me, assessing my preparedness, my trustworthiness.

'It's not about them, not what they look like. It's about me. It's about who we are. What we both see. There's a pact we make in the first few seconds we meet people. Most people miss it. I don't. You should pay attention to it.'

She's awake when she says it. Caffeine awake.

'Okay,' she says, 'when you walked in, what did you think about each of them. Three words.'

'What?'

'Three words to describe Duncan.'

I bite my lips. See his hand resting on the wood of my dad's worktop. His stiff shoulders, his anger that hid his fear. 'Bullish. Jealous. Angry.'

'And Mel?'

Her holding Duncan's arm, guiding him out of my dad's space. The smell of her. And something I can't figure out.

'Protective. Elusive.'

'Protective of you or Duncan?'

'Both. And there was something else too, like she wasn't all here.'

'If you had to name it, that feeling?'

'She was protecting my dad too.'

She picks up my cup. 'More coffee?'

'Isn't it bad for me?'

'Maybe. Want milk instead?'

'No.'

I'd rather have a sister than a mom.

'Thought so.'

Linden is making me alive. Telling me to be alive, be present in these days, be present, remember it all. And I don't know how to do that. How can I do that when already the first few days feel like they've lasted about a second, minutes at most?

I didn't understand Linden until I understood baseball. Since then it has been her and me and baseball.

My first baseball bat, it's nicked and old at the handle like someone has chewed on it with frustration. The neck and length of it are smooth from overuse.

I'm seven and an awkward gangling shambles at my first tryouts. My ignorant hands and untrained eyes. They're stupid for months, if not for the first few years. And the bat seems not to care.

I hate being the new kid, the only girl. With my ridiculous habit of blushing. I stand feeling like I have clothespegs holding me up. I swing at absurd balls, so far out of the zone the catcher has to go chasing the pitch. Of course I miss. Rather spectacularly. The coach and Aunt Linden encourage me, urge me on; my 'peers' yell other things ('girly girl', 'nice swing!'). I strike out in three, none of them strike pitches. The bat slipping from my grip, far too big or stiff or something.

'Well, that was hard to watch,' Aunt Linden says in a way that betrays the fact that whatever she is, she isn't a mother.

'It was even harder to live through.'

'Oh, of course, Roe. Of course.' She laughs and puts her arm around my shoulders.

My dad is at work. Saturday is a busy day for house calls. Saving little old ladies who lock themselves out when they go shopping. My dad thinks I need girl-time. He doesn't think it through when he picks tomboy baseball fanatic Linden to be that girly influence.

Even with the heat of the tryouts still in my face, the taunts following us as we head back to her apartment, I've caught baseball fever.

I spend quite a few nights at Linden's and she starts to take me to a local park and we learn how to play baseball together. She has an eye for these things. For how people move.

Wrigley Field dominates the view out her window and she takes me to loads of games that summer, sitting up in the bleachers, the ivy climbing the wall below us. The seventh inning stretches and Linden talks about Harry Caray and how it just isn't the same without him. Take me out to the ballgame. Holy cow.

When we can't get to the games we watch them on TV, sometimes at our house, sometimes at hers. We become baseball nerds.

'See his tell,' Linden nudges me, beer in hand.

'His shoulder kicks up just on the release,' I say.

'Exactly.'

'And there goes the runner.'

And he's on second. The throw way late.

I'm so determined to show the boys I can do it. So determined to read any pitcher and his tells. That's as much of the secret of batting as your swing, your stance, it's reading what type of pitch is coming your way. That's how I get good. Linden and me, the only girls in the park with mitts and my battered bat and her with her pitch that gets faster and trickier each day. We spend all summer immersed in baseball and well into the fall too. Every day we can, after her classes, my classes. She often stays over at our house, me at hers. Sometimes when she takes me home, it looks as if my dad had never been at the house. And now I know this is the case. These extended weekends with Linden have nothing to do with home games or practicing my base stealing, but have everything to do with the fact that she doesn't have a clue where my dad is.

'I've never been so healthy,' she says as she twirls the bat on the floor encouraging me out of my couch potato slouch. 'Come on Roe, you know you want to.' She doesn't have to ask more than once.

When I'm ten I make the team and every year until I get too tall and lose my co-ordination. I'm still on the team, but my game's off. Avoiding training this winter too.

Now I see grief in her, not when she is still but rather when she moves, doing something routine like frying onions and garlic, which is the base of everything she cooks. She has such clearly emotional hands.

'Shame about the face,' she says when you compliment her.

And she's only half wrong. There's nothing really wrong with her face, it's just that it's not as perfect as her hands and will always be found wanting. I imagine her and her lover, and how it will be the touch of her skilled hands that will turn him on.

And I don't blush when I think these things about her, or anyone. To me it's these moments I want most, where there's nothing between me and the feeling I'm capable of anything.

I imagine us at the table, my dad's beside me and he's talking about keys; I pay attention, I hear the leaving in his voice. I know his tell.

And I make him stay.

Quiz is still taller than me and when I open the door he sweeps me up, lifts me up, and I just hold and hold and hold. He's quiet with me, with his love. How close his breath, my feet still not on the ground. And I think this is what I want, this quiet, but all noise returns when he kisses me and his hands seem to be everywhere and I squirm and Linden clears her throat in the kitchen.

He lets go and then smiles. 'Linden's here?'

'Yup. If you'd given me a chance to say…' I smile and grab his hand. Disappointed and relieved. I don't seem to feel anything simply these days, all emotion comes in pairs, opposites. They rest together: grief and joy; exhaustion and exhilaration; hope and fear.

'You must be Quiz.' Linden shakes his hand, she squeezes his arms. 'You look like a nice boy.' Nice slides out of her like melting butter; she smoulders. I'm horrified and incredibly pleased at the same time.

'Hands off,' I say, 'he's mine.'

'If you insist.'

Quiz blushes, smiles, but doesn't laugh. Oh shit. Not just a social visit then. Linden reaches to the table and grabs her cellphone from her bag, and then her coat from the back of a chair.

'You two go do what you were going to do, I'm going to make some phone calls.' She goes out the back door.

'To her car?'

'Your guess is as good as mine.' But I know what he's here to do, as much as she does.

Quiz leads me to the couch.

'Fess up Roe.'

'What?' I draw it out, my voice scales from low to high.

'My mom's shift finished at 5:30.'

'Good for her, she'll get some family time. Except… you're here.'

'Roe.' Stern.

'Okay, so my dad's not been home for a few days.'

'A missing person's report? He's not just gone away. He's left without telling you.'

'Thanks, Quiz.'

'That's not what I meant.'

'What did you mean?'

He lowers his eyes, all his innocence, all his care, in this simple gesture of consideration.

'That you must be worried. That it must be hard. Harder.'

I take one of his hands and then the other, I open his arms wide, make space. I straddle him. Rub my cheek to his. Mine is smooth and I wonder how that must feel, the smoothness of a girl, the fullness, against his almost stubbled face. My hands slide over his back, rest on his neck. His hands spread out on my back, holding me in place and then they soften and he has me there, enfolded.

The back door swings open, and a rush of cold air races through the room.

'Roe? Quiz?'

Quiz and I separate slowly. With something and nothing changed.

'What's for dinner?' I yell.

'Plain old mac and cheese, with hotdogs. Do you want to join us, Quiz?'

'Yum,' he says, low into my ear. A nibble there, just below, at my nape.

'She's doing the best she can.' I squeeze his hand as we walk into the kitchen.

'I'd love to stay, Linden. Thanks.'

'He absolutely beamed when you told me hands off! That boy's a keeper. Come on, you can tell your Aunt Linden the details.'

But I can't tell her, I don't have the right words.

Quiz goes home, checks in with his mom, goes to his room, and sneaks out of his window to come back here, climbing up the side of the house. He makes a racket and Linden is next door and she knows she should disapprove, but Quiz is just so cute, she's powerless to stop me.

And I'm on top and I'm shaking and the tears fall onto his shoulder, like from the sky. My arms go rigid, but he lifts my hands, folds my arms like they're wings, folds me into him and he holds me. How did this sixteen-year -old boy learn to act like a man? Like a good man?

'Roe.'

It's all soft, the way he says my name. He holds me and shifts us both and it's all elbows and knees and a mess of blankets but we don't giggle. We simply hold onto each other as we disentangle our limbs and realign with him on top. Quiet. Slow. I'm open and folded at the same time. Somewhere I feel something other than grief. For the moment that's enough.

I see us; I'm on my dad's knee, we're at a carnival or something. I'm young. He kisses my face and my hair, tickling my sides, his lips smash out sounds from my grape juice purple lips. I laugh and laugh. I remember my heart beating in my ears. That laugh, his laugh, how he beamed with it. Tears in his eyes.

I put that memory next to the last I have of him. His small smile, his reserved hug and I understand something I had not before: holding back is power. It gives you time to be elusive. To make up your mind to stay or to go.

'Please don't tell anyone,' I say to Quiz, nearly asleep beside me. He takes my finger, pulls it to his lips and kisses it.

'This guy's a sap,' I think.

TUESDAY

In chemistry, Ms Clunes gives us a break from doing experiments. 'A cooling down period.'

Scott, the pyro, is undramatically absent. Rumor has it he's in a daylong detention. Hope there's a psych evaluation thrown in.

'I've been thinking about beauty and grace,' Mr R says. He's sitting at his desk, twirling his beard. His beard that's in need of a trim. Bet his wife used to sit him down in a chair and trim his beard without her top on. Heavy hanging breasts brushing his chin.

'What about truth?' asks Missy.

'No Keats today,' he says. 'Truth is too elusive to speak of here. Today, we're going to talk about spiders.' He flicks off the lights, turns on a video, some nature program he's taped off National Geographic or something. It's on mute, so he can narrate. 'She how she moves? Their lovemaking is quick, slightly clumsy at that.' Most everyone shifts in their seats at the mention of sex, but he doesn't notice. 'But when she devours him, it's all grace and beauty. Deadly, for a minute, chaos, followed by calm.'

'Look, it's Susie Ford,' Freddie points at the screen and shouts, 'I always knew there was something wrong with her!'

Violent departure and then silence.

'I want you to write about a movement of beauty that ends in silence.'

And I want to write about my dad and how he walks, and how the apron straps hang down his back when he cooks, or his smock straps when he works, how he's a fortress, so concentrated and intense and how I'm not there at all in his head or his movements, and yet watching him, over the top of a book or magazine, are moments when he and I are closest. Beauty. Silence.

Then lunch. Then history.

'Where do you think you're going, Miss Davis?' Mr Pavich's voice is steel-sharp, his eyes bore into my back.

'To my seat.' I continue to walk up the aisle.

'Stop!'

I stop but don't turn around.

'Where is your signed test?'

'I forgot.'

'Then you're not welcome in my class. Go to the principal's office.'

It's on principle he's sending me to the principal, because the principal is my pal.

'I can get it for you tomorrow.' My desk is inches away. If I can just sit down, I'll become invisible, he'll leave me alone.

'Not good enough. Go now. Before I give you detentions.'

I'm hot. I want to slap my hands down on his desk and head-butt him. If it didn't mean my forehead would get all greasy. He's either producing slime or he slaps so much grease on to keep his comb-over in place.

'That's not fair.' It's Jess speaking up for me. My heart soars.

'Do you think it was fair when the Serbs stole land from the Croats? When they put them in camps? Raped and murdered them? Was that fair?'

We had to force him into it, but he finally did a bit of actual teaching. He even has a point, but it doesn't mean a thing coming from his mouth. Not enough.

'Outta here,' is all I manage before pushing the door when it should be pulled. My classmates, even though they're on my side, erupt in laughter behind me.

I run my hand over rows and rows of lockers. My hand bouncing out every time I hit the lock and small pull handle. I take my time.

Someone's opened the window in the principal's office. A cut of cold through the room. Miss Stevenson, the secretary, stares me down like I'm Hitler or something.

It was only a test. A stupid test. Who cares?

Mrs Melbourne looks at me rather kindly, my record up until now has been impeccable and she lets me off with a warning and a note to get back into class.

Mr Pavich has pinned up all of our maps and they dangle there from the cork rail that rims the room. They flap in some random draft. I put the note on the table. Mr Creep turns around and rubs his stubby hands together. Picks at his nails, which even I can see are yellowing. Hope he's close to some major illness. Or death.

He hurls dates and names at us, lengthy battles for power, dragging us across vast distances and times, back and forth between countries and alliances. I feel dizzy and sick. My map hangs over his right shoulder and looks like a cauliflower growing out of his ear.

He concludes in the middle of some country's civil war. My notebook is full up with notes. 'One by one I want you to go up to your map and write the grade you think you deserve on it. And tell us why.' There's a thick black marker we each need to use.

Jess is first. As always. She picks up the pen and swings her hips up to her map.

'I should get an A,' Jess says. 'Because it's stunning and correct. See this here, this bit of coast? You'll notice the dual shades because for sixteen days in May 1943 it fell into enemy hands before being reclaimed.'

My best friend the suck-up.

I'm last, his system for hanging these horrible things, crystal clear. From the left side of his head, round the room, down the grade-scale, to my cauliflower. The little shit. I'm really calm to start with but then my heart beats and beats. I have something important to say, but don't know how to say it, when to say it. How to make a controversial point.

'I should get a C,' I say, after Veronica Sampson hands me the pen. Her D, clear and defeated on her map. She's just one of many in the class willing to put themselves down in public. Life's too short to be a good girl.

I write a big black 'C' on my map. 'Because I've worked really hard, I've listened to the scant information actually taught, I tape record the class, listen to it later, with a map in front of me, have forty pages of notes for this term alone. I'm smart too. I think my map is less perfect than it should be because,' and this is where I know I step over a line, 'the teaching sucks.'

He says nothing. Goes with his smug red pen and over the front of each map he scrawls our grades. Jess gets a B, as punishment for standing up for me, even though her map is first up on the wall and a couple of A- scores follow hers. And her perfect map is ruined. He moves around the vicious circle, on down the scale until mine.

'And this, Miss Davis, is a perfect detail of an amoeba.' And he writes an easy 'F' and his hand hovers and he finishes it off with a long dash. He's given me an F minus. Another made up grade. Made up for maximun public humiliation.

'Well done, Colonel Pavich,' I say standing at the door between a slow death and freedom. I start to clap my hands, slow, loud. 'You've created a dictatorship.'

The bell rings.

I hope my dad comes home tonight so I never ever have to come back to this class.

Jess laughs as she pulls me down the hall. 'You're in the shit now.'

'Sorry he punished you too.'

'Down with Hitler,' she says. Then she opens her mouth wide and mocks teeth being pulled out. 'Speaking of which, have a great time at the dentist.'

I don't have a note for this either. Too bad.

'See ya later.' I say and run to my locker, put my hands out to protect myself from all the crap that threatens to fall. Grab my coat, shove all my crap back in and walk calmly through the exit least likely to be watched over.

The bus rides low and slow to the station and I start here with the end of the line: Linden (an aunt, a tree, a train station). Any journey I take on these trains starts or ends with family. Starts and ends with family. Travels through family too. Is this what fate has in for me? That I pass through these people who have adopted me, every time I try to get home?

Linden is the first stop on the Purple Line, with a platform enclosed on three sides; I sit on the train and wait for us to move. The heat isn't on yet and I'm frozen despite my long underwear and my coat which reaches my thighs and the hat which everyone tells me will keep in the heat but only makes my head itch.

Doors closing.

Welcome to Purple Line run 511.

Central is next.

In the direction of travel, doors open on the left at Central.

The announcements are on some sort of de-personalized loop. A male voice, metallicized as it works its way through the system and out the speakers.

The Metra train, the posh train, passes through Central too, a few blocks west. And at Davis, two more stops on, (*doors open on the right at Davis*) the Metra is close enough to touch. We used to get off at Davis to go to our dentist on Church Street. Now I get off at Dempster, because it's closer to the high-rise building he's in now, which always smells like burning rubber.

I get off the train. Visit the third generation dentist so young I can't believe he's out of high school. He must be. I've got one cavity at the back, have to go back next week. I say no to the whitening option.

Back at the station. The pigeon-shit makes the platform sticky. Humans fight for space with the birds beneath the heater.

My dad and I must be the only people on the north shore who use the train regularly, who don't drive everywhere.

'Your grandpa was a fanatic,' dad says, as though he's any different. 'I just like to ride the 'El' for the joy of it. It's a habit.'

'It's an obsession, dad.'

'Maybe.'

And Peter Berwyn Davis doesn't care. He pushes kids and elderly women out the way to get the first seat on the train, up by the driver.

'The first real view of the city is just before you hit Howard.' All change at Howard. 'The Hancock Building comes into view. Right there.' My dad always points straight ahead, as if he was in the front car. 'Best seats in the house.' He says of the front, 'I often have to sit next to the professional train riders, smelling of groin sweat.'

'Oh, dad, too much information.'

'But it's true,' he says. 'Mustier than armpit sweat, which is there too. And old piss. The piss on the floor and I always think that it's awfully mean because the drivers are right there, and some guys just whip it out and take a pee on the floor.'

'Dad!'

'Don't be such a girl. A body is a body is a body.'

'But it's gross.'

'Maybe a bit. But that's life. Remember the time you knocked out your front teeth?'

'Of course.'

'It hurt, right?'

'You bet. And gross too.'

'Well, the world is like this: blood and guts and pain. It may not be pretty, but it's real.'

'And why is that better?'

'Because you know you're alive.'

Between our house and Mrs Morse's, a footpath cuts down to a small cove of sand. It's a private beach and teenagers go down there drinking all the time. It used to be that if Old Mrs Morse liked them (if they left cold beer on her porch) she'd let them alone, but if they took a leak in her forsythia or her roses, she'd call the cops.

Our beach comes in and out of fashion. Some years we have weekend after weekend of partying, barbaric yawps, of bonfires, of couples arguing outside my window. One year a car doesn't stop at the end of the road and goes over the ravine.

It plows between our houses, goes right through and out into the air like a cartoon car with no road under it, and out over the edge, taking one of the oldest maples with it. The driver, a girl, drunk, and only a handful of days past sixteen, dies when the steering wheel goes right through her body, and the driver's seat, and ends up in the backseat.

Old Mrs Morse is furious about the tree. Everyone else says what a shame about the girl. 'Just stupid,' Mrs Morse says. 'Just stupid. She knew the risks. She took them. I hear she fought for the damn car keys. A dumb kid. The world is a safer place without her.'

For months skid marks darken the road and turn into deep welts in the mud after the curb and cut all the way to the edge.

'We have no idea how she got up the speed to do it.'

'I'm telling you,' Old Mrs Morse says, 'it was suicide.'

A big crane comes and pulls up the car. The lake water is way back and the car isn't even wet. Its bumper had wrapped around a tree and there are branches stuck out of the windows, sand falling from its front fender.

I wonder about the girl. Was she stupid? Or did she know exactly what she was doing?

When I get home from the dentist, Mrs Morse's house is alive with sunlight. It bounds off the windows throughout the house. The big space inside is reeling with the light. Even without her inside, without her grey braid swinging, her old strong frame, it's still hers. I shove my hand down the side of the couch, bring the keys up in bunches. Within minutes of going outside the metal is cold through my pockets.

Dad and I try to create some sort of order at Mrs Morse's house but we're not putting in the time. A few bags of clothes to the Salvation Army and that's about it. Her year of absence, and every time I'm inside all I can think about is how it smells of her.

It is hers.

In the last few days in her house, the water torments Old Mrs Morse, with the heavy waves crashing in the dark, the roots of the trees creaking, pulling the house towards the shore. I stay with her a few nights, join her while she paces and rants. I put out my arm and she hooks her own through it. Her thin white nightdress. And a thick robe that must be her husband's. And I wrap it around her, and she's warmer but smells musty and looks more senile. And I'm sorry I've done it. I try not to have this image of her when I think of her, try not to remember her calling me Peter, because I want to believe that the Village kills her when they send her away, when she can take care of herself. But those nights, I'm not sure what I find more frightening, the roaring of the lake, or her ranting.

To live in fear of what might happen. She'd been living with small fears for years. But near the end, the big fear takes over: in the middle of the night you can never be sure what might happen.

She wears her long hair braided, usually just a single braid, but sometimes tucked up inside a hat, if she'd been gardening; she's held onto her beauty like other older people have not.

'It's this house,' she says, 'it keeps me young. There's magic at the door when you step through. My dad built it that way.'

'The Village wants this land,' she says, 'and I'd half give it, if it didn't mean giving up this house.'

Over the years, I play along the shore with the rest of the kids, wading with my trousers turned up. A hatred of the water like lead in the ball and socket of my hip. Not the idea of water, not water from a distance, but of the sand-grit reality of it. The inconvenience. The unpredictability. Hatred, not fear. And now it's part of me. In the summer I go down to the cove, always faking bravado when Dad's there. When I go alone I scoot timidly, on my butt, over the rocks, down the dirt slide. I pick my way among the detritus of Milwaukee's trash. The breaker rocks down there are supposed to stop more erosion and I guess they're doing their job even as used condoms and maxi-pads get stuck in the deep crevices carved out as the water advances and recedes in different years.

I walk to the edge of the ravine and look out. The ice as thick as I've ever seen it. The moon thin as I've ever seen it. The city glows red to the south, and somehow, from somewhere, there's light. I've never known a place so quiet. I walk over to Mrs Morse's house.

These days I'm afraid. I admit it. I have keys, one of which must be hers. When she was alive I could go over anytime and her back door would be unlocked. But now, since she died, dad keeps her keys. Last year, at the beginning of spring, the Village put up bright police tape to keep people out, like it was the scene of a crime, a murder. My dad ripped it down as soon as they'd gone.

'We don't need to advertise that it's empty.'

Don't need to advertise that it will be brought low.

The winter shadow of the house spills down the ravine. Its plunge is sudden, unbearable. I couldn't find the flashlight, so I've grabbed dad's headlamp instead, the one he wears to Mrs Morse's when he's working over there.

No new snow since Sunday night. It's all crystalline and crunches beneath my boots. I used to walk on snow like this, its crusty top sometimes an inch thick. And me, light on my feet, walking across, above the ground. 'I'm walking on water!' I yell.

Me, thinking myself clever.

Today the crust breaks again and again. With each step.

I zigzag my feet to find the safest spaces on the steps. The planks, once sealed and painted a steel grey blue, have buckled and look sickly and flesh-like between the cracked paint. The steps run parallel to the house, the planks of the porch come out at perpendicular angles and you can see the rough convex bits where water has buckled the wood. Splinters in your feet in the summer. Slippery covered in ice. I put my arms out to the side for balance.

Her front door is locked. I don't need to try the handle to know it.

The de-icer clanks in my pocket, against her keys. Of course I'll have to use it. Acrid, harsh fumes flit up my nose and freeze there. I have a feeling I'll wake up in the middle of the night, smelling like a factory. Smelling more than a bit like Linden.

I spray some de-icer on the keys, on the single lock on Old Mrs Morse's front door and I wonder how she got away with that, living next door to my dad for so long. But she did. I have at least ten possible keys, on different rings. Now that I'm here, I can clearly disregard a few without even trying them. Lever keys when this is a simple pin-tumbler Yale. All the keys are copies, so they don't really match the feel of the lock.

The door would be easy to kick in, but it's on principle that I go through key after key. I wouldn't be my dad's daughter if I resorted to force.

The key that finally opens the door is a rough fit. A bad copy, years old. I wonder if my dad's other copy is better because this one's a travesty.

I've not been in this house for months and as the door swings open, creaks on winter hinges, it's still like death in there.

My toes remain outside, on the door-stop, and I pull my hand back. The last of the day's light slants weakly through the house from west to east, dark racing on its heels.

I step through, into her house, for the first time since my dad left. I am looking for something. A reason maybe, although an answer would be better.

The keys are heavy in my pocket, the space of the house open before me. The house is still, arctic.

I take out my headlamp. It makes the world even stranger. All the peripheral information is lost. Light to pitch to lost.

I turn from side to side, light sweeping like a lighthouse. Must look creepy from outside but no one will be watching.

I don't know where to begin. Don't know where to look. What am I looking for? Things lost? Things to be lost? Precarious or precious? Solid or safe?

This house is anything but abandoned. If anything it's been loved too much, if that's possible. With everything Mrs Morse had to give and Dad too.

And now it's waiting for them to come back. And no one else will do.

I stand in the hall. The stairs straight ahead, the living room to the right, the dining room that leads to the kitchen to the left. I head towards the kitchen. Start with the familiar. Not one to waste space, she built a bookcase beneath the stairs. It's jammed not with books, but with old bills, letters and old *TIME* magazines. Dusty, slightly damp lumps. The dust has become dirt and what had once been cleanly delineated sheets of paper has mâchéd into pulp.

We've never cleaned the house. It's part of why I feel bad. I should have felt bad about all of this well before now. Totally bad. Curl up in a ball bad about losing Mrs Morse. Instead we've just left all her cherished chaos to rot.

The house smells like her, like earth, and her gardening gloves still flop over a nail near the back door. The frame is a grey-blue, well-weathered, cracked and chipped. Her kitchen counters are wide appliance-free expanses, her fridge is in our house now, cranking away. No power in here anymore. A shovel rests by the back door too. We've killed all her plants. Maybe it's the move, maybe it's grief.

'You need to remember where you've come from,' dad says. 'I helped build this house with my own hands. Remember that. These calloused, key-cutting hands built this. And it matters.'

I'm remembering so much it hurts. The dust on all the surfaces is untouched. The saved door still stands, mounted, in the middle of the living room, aloof. I try to imagine what my dad has built in this house, what he fixes when he spends time here. How does this house touch him?

What makes him love this place? And love Mrs Morse?

I used to play hide and seek here all the time. Open and close the door. Step through into another world. Shouting to Mrs Morse to play a king or a princess or a queen bee. And she does, she steps through into my world, raises and lowers her voice, crinks her fingers.

I run my gloved hands up part of the frame, across the beveled surface, to the handle. I look closely, rust clings to the edges of the lock, which looks tight and strong, even unlocked. I can't bring myself to turn the handle.

I need it to open easily. To stay intact. I need WD40.

Down in the basement the cobwebs are peaceful. Older than a year old. Decades old. A workbench, with hammers hanging from makeshift holds, big drawers with metal crescent handles, plastic containers with tiny drawers for all sorts of nails and screws and fittings.

Chandeliers of cobwebs decorate the ceiling and what looks to be an abandoned wasps' nest hugs a corner by the outer wall. Mrs Morse wasn't a dress-up sort of grandmotherly type. She was a 'let's thin out this jungle that my back yard has become' type and would hand you an axe or a shovel. 'Let's paint this.' 'Cut this down.' 'Plant this.'

Elizabeth Reeder

The headlamp flickers, I hit it with my hand, and it goes out completely. There's just enough light from outside to outline the door. I'm up the stairs in a flash and then I'm outside Mrs Morse's house with pitch black space behind me. I look at the lights next door, coming from our house. The windows lit up bright like a face. What was I thinking, all that brightness is the opposite of a beacon. It's garish. Intrusive.

Who would want to go back there?

Inside our house the answering machine light flashes. One message. My heart in my throat. I trail snow and cold across the room. Press the button.

'Roe, Linden. It's Officer Berg here, Quiz's mom. Can you call us at the police station? There's been some activity on Peter's Visa card. We'd like to talk to you about it.'

I call her back. His card has been used downtown, then in Champaign.

'We don't know what to think,' Mrs Berg says. 'Does he know anyone there? Is there any reason he'd be at the U of I?'

No reason I can think of. I call Linden. She's on her way home. Another voice in the car.

'That's strange,' she says. 'U of I? Really?'

'She said it could have been stolen.'

'From Peter? Where? How?'

'I just don't know. All the activity was on Saturday, early Sunday and nothing since.'

'God. I hope he's okay.'

Don't we all.

Just before midnight, I'm lying in bed, trying to hear everything and nothing at the same time.

Where is the water beneath the ice or the wind ripping through the winter-bare trees? I can't hear either.

'He was lonely at my place,' Linden had said earlier tonight of big red-headed Ken. A hunk. 'You sure it's okay if he stays over?'

Of course, I wasn't going to get in her way. And now, only four days after my dad's gone and only the second night that Linden's slept in his bed—the noises, the gasps of pleasure. The bedframe hitting the wall. In a rhythm of sorts. There's loud that wakes you up, sudden, sharp, and then there's loud that wakes you up and keeps you up.

I've tried just hanging out and letting them finish. It just doesn't seem like they're going to finish anytime this century. I try to listen closely and learn stuff, but what can you learn from a groan? My head's pounding. School again tomorrow and they're not making any effort at all to keep the racket down.

There's a crash. I'm guessing that it's my dad's Black Label Bottle bedside light. Nothing stops. It's ridiculous. And it goes on. The duration of it, it's inhuman. Where did Linden find this guy?

I put the pillows over my head and they mask but do not silence the racket coming from across the landing.

If Mrs Morse was here she'd be pounding on the front door. 'Keep it in your pants, so the rest of us can get some sleep.' I'm making this up, obviously, she'd never had any occasion that I know of to talk like that, but I can see her, long gray braid sliding down one side of her ankle length parka, bare feet stuffed into decade-old boots, nightgown showing beneath her coat, loose hair a tassle at the end.

I imagine the boys who frequent the beach lining up, climbing up the side of our house for a peep show. Whooping, 'Give it to her,' 'Ride her baby.' And shouting 'Finally' when, if, they ever stop the racket.

I can't bear to stay here any longer. Listening to her escape what there is no escaping. I get dressed, long johns under my jeans, just in case I find myself outside and exposed to the elements. I avoid the creaking third stair and the broken first one. The house is not pitch black, but gently dark, the hint of a moon coming through the windows, the reflecting snow magnifying and diffusing the sliver of light. Peaceful. Whole. Complete. Sad maybe. Out the window the lake and sky are one. I slide my finger under the keys to the Honda, flip them off the key holder. I've seen the movies, I've had four lessons, have wanted to drive since forever, I know how to do this. I hoist the garage door open in a jerk and then a smooth slide and push. Linden's car parked behind our Honda is too close. I go back inside. Her bag is on the table (along with half a dozen empty beer bottles), I shake it, hear the rattle of keys. Fish them out.

Outside I breathe on them, rub them between my hands and slide them into the nearly frozen lock. It turns, the door creaks and I hold it open to listen for any change to the sounds inside the house. Reliable gasps and I'm reassured. I slide in, move the seat up slightly to fit my legs. Pray that it will start. That her car's got a quiet start.

I've seen the movies. I reverse out without the lights, in fact I wait until the end of the street before I turn them on. Full beam. I brake, fiddle with knobs and get normal beams. A rush, stomach, pulse. Thrill and fear wave through me.

I need to know where I'm going, where I'm heading. I pull up to Jess's house, and text her. She comes to the window. Holds up two fingers, minutes and peace. Then she's at the window and sliding down the eaves, landing in the convenient pile of snow at the bottom.

She holds onto her shoes and runs up to the car in her bare feet. Manages to keep a grip with her toes on the ice.

'Whose car?'

'Linden's.'

'You continue to surprise me, Ms Davis.'

I continue to surprise myself.

She plays with the radio. Finds something that'll do. Blasts it. Puts her feet up against the heater, her red toenails unaffected by her sprint.

'This is not like you at all,' she says.

'Meet the new me.'

I pull out and start to head for the Edens.

'Take Ridge,' she says.

Jess is across from me in the booth at Ray's Diner, smooshing faces with a guy named Patrick. I'm on the outside edge of the table, Patrick's friend Joe is trying to get his hand under across my lower back but I know his ultimate target is my bra strap. How high school.

He's not ugly but he smells like armpits and teenage boy. I'm scanning the room for escape. There's a cough. A guy at the counter looks up and nods his head to the waitress who brings over more coffee. I kick Jess and she kicks back hard but doesn't respond. I wonder if I clipped Patrick by mistake.

Joe's fingers are walking, sticky over my back. I sit forward, reaching for sugar and then sit back hard. There's a crack of bone against the vinyl'd back. But not a sound from Joe. He must be a real man. Within seconds the advance has continued.

'Get a load of that geek,' he says, punching Patrick across the table. Up goes a finger.

This guy walks by the window and pushes at the door with his shoulder.

He's got on old style, straight-cut Levi's, cuffs turned up, polished black shoes (no steel tip), double breasted leather coat, cut short just to his waist, neat hips, red scarf and a cashmere fedora, with the back turned up. Totally retro.

'Excuse me,' I say, not even turning to bra-strap guy. I slide out. Jess doesn't even look up. I take myself to the bathroom. On my way back fedora guy smiles at me. It's not an offer and I don't care. I sit down across from him. He's watched me cross the room and raises an eyebrow when I fold myself and my legs into the seat.

'You got enough room under there?'

I realize that I'd completely missed his silky purple waistcoat. I grin. 'My pal's sucking the face off some guy and she's left me with Mr Roving-Hands.'

'There's plenty of other tables.' He's serious. His eyes jump to other tables and then back to me.

I settle back into the seat. 'You can't expect a sixteen-year-old to sit alone.'

'Is that something you save for us twenty-somethings?'

'You don't look alone. You look content. Solitary.'

'How do you know that I'm not waiting for someone?'

'Well, are you?'

'Yes, actually.'

'Who then?'

'The love of my life.'

Cruising, he's cruising and he's not kicked me away from his table. Good sign. And then I notice all the other signs and while I'm not exactly sure what tips the scales, and although it should have been the hat or the way he walked, or the very neatness of him, what really makes it click for me is the fact that as he speaks one of the hottest guys I've ever seen walks by and this guy, Fedora Man, forgets that anything else in the universe exists.

'For the man of your dreams,' I say, missing a beat, but not two.

'He'll walk in that door at any moment. I'll know it's him.'

'Is that him?'

'No, I've already had him. He's fine. But a screamer. No harm in looking though.'

It's hot and sudden and my face is burning.

'So you think you'll just know when he walks in? Is that the way it works?'

'Sometimes. They usually leave more quietly than they arrived. Except for the breakers.'

'Heartbreakers?

'Not always the same thing. No, the loud ones break everything on the way out.'

Those are the ones my aunt goes for. She's got one at home I think...

'What type are you?' I ask.

'I'm a left behind.'

'Me too.'

'I thought you'd be a leaver.'

'Really? So far I'm a left behind.'

'I'm sorry to hear that Ms...' he holds out his hand, as if to have me kiss it, then changes his mind.

'Roe,' I say. His grip is strong, cool and honest.

'Like the deer?' he asks.

'Yup.'

'How did your mom know about those legs?'

'She didn't. "Hooves hard as hammers" was the phrase she used about me. Or so I've heard.'

'Jake,' he says.

I order some eggs and bacon. He gets a coffee. We share a short stack. He drowns them in syrup. Just like I like it.

'So you're aiming for San Fran?'

'It's my Zion,' Jake says. 'Chicago is my fallback city.'

'It's not a bad second.'

He shrugs. 'But still, always, second. Better than LA, but not Mecca. With these winters, no wonder. Shit, it's not natural.'

He swears like it's a gentle, held-in sneeze. His smile is all cheeks, inherently full of mischief. His thin jeans, his open-necked jacket. His decorative scarf. No wonder he's freezing.

'What would you do if you moved there?' I ask.

'I'd sell my body.'

'No, I mean to make money.'

'Ouch.'

'What do you do here?'

'Stuff. What about you?'

'I go to school. I steal my aunt's car in the middle of the night when she's having loud sex across the hall. Oh yeah, and I'm left.'

'By who?'

'My dad left home last Friday and hasn't been home since.'

'No kidding.'

'He wasn't a breaker. He was a slitherer. Not a peep. Not a warning.'

'How's your mom about it?'

'How would I know? She left when I was a month old.'

His face has fallen. His hands flat on the table. Face down but open.

'Bummer,' he says.

'Big bummer.' I laugh.

He turns one palm over. Wiggles his fingers. I put my hand palm down over his. Wriggle my middle finger. He wiggles back.

'Phi Beta Kappa handshake,' he says.

'Huh?'

'It's a secret society.'

He turns his hand over, traps mine. I extricate myself.

'So where do you think he's gone?'

'Who?'

'Your dad.'

'I thought you were talking about the man of your dreams.'

'Stop stalling and answer the question.'

'I don't know. He left to travel or to find a key or something.'

'The key to what?'

'How the hell should I know?' Louder than I should have. Softer. 'To this door he inherited.'

Jake's lips are together, rueful eyes down and a smile grows.

'That's stupid,' he says.

I laugh. Even if it seems this way from the outside, it's only half true. From the inside it's maddening. 'It sort of makes sense if you know him.'

'What? It makes sense to leave his daughter?'

'I can look after myself.'

He looks around the diner. It's 2:30am. Most of the men look like truckers. The other men look like Jake and the pretty boy sitting at the bar. Jess and I are the only girls. Jess and Patrick are taking a breath. She gives me the thumbs up. I wish I knew a sign for good-looking but gay as hell. I have Quiz. But now I'm glad to have had Jake for an hour or so.

'Aren't you a cute one,' Jess says, she's suddenly by my elbow; her breath, still smelling like Patrick, is hot on my neck.

'I think we'll be going.' I unfold myself and go to put some money on the table. Jake closes my hand around the bills.

'You're a swan, Miss Roe,' Jake purrs, and adds a whistle and a wow. 'I'll catch the bill.'

'Thanks, Mr Jake. You're no ugly duckling yourself.'

On Lake Shore Drive the ice is solid except for one broken crevice near the graveyard, the rows of tombstones you can see from the 'El', just before Howard. And it's here that the water churns black and splashes over the rocks and onto the road trying to get into the graves on the other side. Jess has her feet up on the dash, her hands shoved on either side, near the vents.

Jess. Even as she's seeking heat in this arctic zone, she's all summer. Her bright red toenails, perfect. I feel the heat of our summers together and this one coming. How she'll pull me forward towards the sun and I'll let her. It's all along my bones.

I turn off the radio and she doesn't protest. We pass the Baha'i and the sky all dark behind it. I pull into Gilson Park.

'Come on. Let's go look at the ice.'

'Do we have to?'

'Yes,' I say, and drag her there, draping her in a blanket from the car. I don't even want to think what might be on it—who knows what Linden gets up to in the backseat.

The moon barely brushes the surface of the lake that is thick and gnarled with snow and ice and sand and dirt.

We sit a bit up from the shore, in snow-covered grass.

'He's gone.' I say.

'Who?'

'My dad, Jess, he's gone.'

'What, for the night or something? Is that why Linden's there?'

'No, Jess, he's disappeared.'

She pulls her feet into a cross-legged position, leans toward me and turns my face towards her. My eyes always go red like a baby's before I cry. And my lips go tight like a turtle's pinched face when I'm so upset I can't really speak.

'No turtle yet, Roe, but I see that you may be telling a truth.' And then she hits me. Hard, on the arm.

'Ow.'

'That's for not telling me.' And then she lies down and pulls me down beside her. Wraps me in the blanket with her, and gives me a good hug. 'And this is because it sucks.'

I don't cry. I just rest for a few minutes next to Jess. Glad she knows.

'Where do you think he is?' she asks.

'His credit card was used downtown and in Champaign before he got smart and realized it'd be tracked.'

'Why'd he be down there?'

'I have no idea.'

I drop her off at the corner near her house. She's going to have to risk opening the door. For the return journey she has shoes on. I turn off my lights as I enter the road. But the game's up. The house is ablaze, the kitchen light on, and through the window I see Linden sitting at the table.

If she smoked, she'd have a full ashtray in front of her. Post-coital, pre-parental.

She rubs the end of her index finger with her thumb. Her head down, only her eyes lifting at the last minute. 'And so it begins. The teenage angst.'

It doesn't feel like angst, it just feels like it's suppose to feel.

'Don't try to be a mother, Linden. It won't suit you.'

She looks up. Her face is lined, drawn like a mother's. But that's not enough. A mom would be doing things differently. Be swaying with her own grief. Something. Something Linden isn't doing. A mom would be putting me first. I guarantee it.

'You're right.'

'You two were sure rocking the house with your loving.'

She laughs. 'You should have knocked or something.'

'Like you'd have heard. Why should I get in the way of your fun?'

'Because it's your house? I'm sorry, Roe.'

'Don't be. I'm not. Your car handles the ice nicely.'

'Thank you. Car Talk's best suggested number one. For lesbians actually, but who's to say they should get all the good cars? It's got new tires too, snow tires.'

Whoopee, snow tires.

She takes her feet off the table and sits forward, open-legged, she's dressed for the elements all the way down to her boots. Playing it more calm than she'd felt when she'd discovered her car, and then me, gone. She was just about to come looking.

'So where'd you go?'

'Nowhere.'

'So where did that nowhere look like?'

'Like the inside of a diner.'

'What'd you have?'

'Eggs, bacon, a short stack.'

'Coffee?'

'Nope. I'm still a growing kid, I should cut back.'

'Roe, it's only three more weeks until you can take your test. Do me a favor, don't do it again.'

'You going to keep the noise down?'

But she doesn't promise and neither do I.

WEDNESDAY

The train makes a sound like a heartbeat, like breath. It rattles. It rocks from side to side, balanced on the cusp of toppling over as it takes a curve fast, almost too fast.

Some trains tilt. Dad once read out a bit of an article about these trains that actually tilt so they can take the curves faster, like a plane banking left or right, like a speed boat creating a huge wake, its rump right up there in the air. It doesn't seem right on a train.

This train leans, creaking the whole time and shudders back and forth as it rights itself.

It's the express, the Purple Line Express to downtown. Stations fly past or we fly past, on a middle track, one set of rails away from the Red Line which makes every stop, and holds memory after memory, song after song. I don't know what to sing today. If I can sing today.

Dylan for Davis.

Tears for Fears at Howard.

Chicago at Chicago.

Last spring, opening home game, no one beside me at the coveted front seat up by the driver, facing forward. The whole city before me. Lots of people behind me. At South Boulevard, just before the Hancock comes into view for the first time, I give up my seat to a small boy in a Cubs t-shirt and mini-mitt. His mom encourages manners.

'What do you say, Tom?'

'Thank you.'

She nods too. 'Thank you.'

I sit on the flat seats facing sideways, where I can still glimpse where we're going. In front of me stands a man with thick thighs, solid, full waist, no beer belly, flat Midwestern accent. His young, slightly trashy wife, who's wearing sweatpants and a sweatshirt, sits on a seat as he sings to his son who is slung on his back like a sack of potatoes, in a child-sack, rucksack.

I am meeting Linden outside the main gate. She'll walk over from her apartment.

Addison is next.

The doors open on the right at Addison.

The mechanical voice.

And then the driver, 'GO CUBS!'

The husband and wife argue.

'You aren't taking him to a game, not in this temperature.'

'What are you talking about? Look at that sun. I most certainly am taking my son to the game. Right over there.' He points. Wrigley Field dominates the horizon. His legs are wide, supporting him as he stays standing despite the rocky jerking movement of the train.

'The sun may be shining but it's wild out there. Look at those flags whip.'

The husband with the baby slung on his shoulders, holds onto the rail and leans back, forty-five degrees, the baby dangling free, arms and legs floppy, head supported by the sling, grinning.

'Stop that Daryl. Right now.'

Their son's bare legs. What are they on the train for if not to go to the game? Everyone on this train is going to the game, except for the poor folks who have to go to work. What illusion was she under when she got on the train? Diaper bag slung over her shoulder. Her husband's Cubs hat, and jacket. The Cubs milk bottle her son is holding?

Addison is next.

'Go Cubs!' says the driver, again.

'We're getting off. Getting tickets.' He swings himself and the baby around to face the doors. They slide open.

This is Addison.

She kicks her leg up and hustles herself from the seat. I don't get up off my seat until the last minute.

I follow them. Wrigley Field right there. People look like ants, brightly colored ants, milling among the seats. The sky is blue, blue, blue.

Doors closing.

Belmont is next.

Their son is rosy-cheeked from the heat of the train. The husband walks first, ahead, she's three paces behind, dragging her heels. He takes a step forward and turns back towards her in one fluid, generous movement; his grin open like his arms. His son on his back mimics him.

'It's the first home game of the season. How can we not go?'

'We can't, not.'

And she kisses her son first, rubs his leg and her hand slips smoothly down her husband's side and around over his solid, his sexy, ass.

Linden is at the ballpark with her 'Home Run Queen' shirt clinging to her tits. She's the Sweetheart of Swing. Tight jeans and she looks sexy as hell. She could be going to this game with just about anyone, having springtime sex, first bud love, before or after the game, hell I'm sure she could find a corner somewhere to have a quickie in the park if the urge caught her, and her man. Something not meant to last until summer or even until the lilies of the valley, full bloom.

Instead, she's going with me. It's always vaguely upsetting that she dresses more sexily than me, far more skimpily. And that she carries it off better than I ever could. Hers is a fitted t-shirt. Mine's a big boxy one that looks good on no one but the guys who buy four beers at a time and transfer them into their brought-from-home gallon plastic cups.

We're in the bleachers. How can it not be the bleachers?

How can we do anything but smile, on a day like this?

Our team is at home. 2-1 in the first away games. Not perfect, but pretty darn good. The day couldn't be better, the bluest sky. And it's not as cold as it could be.

The baby will be just fine.

The flags fly, the seats are full. All of our foolish hope. The Cubs here, all new, with all the possibility in the world.

This year there might be world peace.

This year we'll end world hunger and poverty.

This year Linden will let me have some of her beer.

This year the Cubs will win the World Series.

And now, today, ten months later, I know none of these things are true.

Will be true. I know other things are true.

I'm flunking history.

I've got a pyromaniac lab partner.

I'm officially no longer a virgin.

And I may be (and day by day it feels more and more like a possibility) a real, live, abandoned kid.

Today the sky is blue. Snow clings to the gutters, frost too, thick on the windows on the edge of the train platforms where there are no heat lamps. Under the lamps pigeons and people crowd together. The train moves fast, almost too fast. And I'm on it.

Then the John Hancock towers ahead. Turning from toy-sized to skyscraper. Lightning rods, undeniable, necessary.

The Purple Line goes straight, with small curves, until downtown crowds in close.

Merchandise Mart.

And as we loop the loop, east, south, west, north, we visit presidents: Madison, Adams, Quincy, Washington (and the presidents we don't visit, Monroe, Jackson, Harrison, Roosevelt—Clinton wasn't named after that Clinton...). And then I get off at Washington and loop the loop the other way on the Brown Line.

Clark and Lake is next.

Doors open at the right at Clark and Lake.

Transfer to green, orange and blue line trains at Clark and Lake.

City Hall and Thompson Center.

And even though I've already been to this stop and not got off the train, this time I do. At Clark. On the platform there's a high pitched screech here, like at Howard. Birds of prey to scare the pigeons. People look up. They're the visitors, residents know better. Boxed nature.

I head underground. Get disoriented. An escalator, unbound, uncoiled. Workmen standing where steps should be, segment after segment peeled back. I crane my neck, look back. Something broken, broken open.

Down further there's a shift. People with luggage. Signs for O'Hare; that's where I'm going. Did dad come this way too? Blue line towards O'Hare, it feels counter-intuitive. O'Hare feels west, south even, but the picture looks like it's to the north.

There's a theory of subway maps, like the London Underground. Dad tells me.

'They draw the maps to make the area seem smaller and more manageable. To bring the suburbs further in. Make them more attractive for homebuyers. So it's totally distorted. In some places you can ask tourists to travel between two stops and they might try and change trains two or three times, it could take them an hour, with half a mile of walking up stairs, down stairs within the subway system. By foot, out in the real world, it'd be five minutes, a couple hundred metres. No perspective.'

And down here, my pocket CTA train map in hand, he's right. I'm heading towards O'Hare (west and south), but it doesn't feel logical for where I'm going, which is north again.

The Flat Iron Building, filling the blunt ended triangled corner, is right there when I get off the train. The frost makes all the buildings lighter, glisten in the sun. These three streets meeting at an intersection, going off and coming from six directions, not a spaghetti junction, just a crazy one. Where Chicago's grid system meets the meandering diagonals of Clark, Lincoln and Milwaukee that follow old Potowatamee trails which in turn followed glacial fault lines.

'Hard left or soft left?' Linden will often ask into the phone when she's driving. Directions given, cell smooshed to her shoulder, amber lights cavalierly ignored. My life in her hands. 'Hard or soft?' she yells. We careen, cars honk, but we're safely through and, amazingly, usually, on the right street. Part of me is convinced she loves the drama of it.

Where else but here are there streets like these? Buildings that fill corners which aren't corners but triangles, all these sides. Creative spaces.

I'm desperately hungry. Linden's talked about places around here. I spot a place that looks great, with a long chalked list of breakfast burritos, three-egg omelets, giant cups of coffee. Veggie options in green, meat options in red, with dripping letters.

A smart café. Literally. Everyone reading vintage classic paperbacks, working on powerbooks, smoking roll-ups.

Not what you'd expect here. Or maybe they're all just being arty in a smoky Sartre sort of way.

I sit at a table by the window. Bacon, sausages, scrambled eggs on their way. Double tall dark roast already hot in my hands. City snow is dirty almost as it falls. Exhaust grey.

The eggs are perfect. The bacon, crisp. The bathroom is painted black, long and wide, with a single white bulb. Too dark to see the damage of the

Elizabeth Reeder

night before. If there is damage from the night before.

Yesterday morning Quiz had left at dawn to get home for his mother's hot pancakes and real maple syrup. Perfect family. Probably have a tree out back with a tap for summer sap.

This morning was short: after a couple hours of sleep, Linden got up at the crack of dawn, went to her studio. Me up not so early, faking my walk to school, texting Jess telling her I was ditching school. Invitation implicit. Her disbelief too.

Really?

Good girl Roe goes off the rails.

Yes, really.

Good for you, she texts back.

Me relieved when she doesn't show up at the station. And now here. Desperate to have her in front of me, making me laugh. Who wants to be alone all day with their thoughts?

I pull my scarf across my face, my breath turns the inside hot and damp against my face. I walk up Milwaukee and then turn left onto West Canton. I know this route well. The houses define it.

Mrs Morse's house has an elaborately carved sandstone front, with peaks and gargoyles. A bunch of houses out here look just like hers. My dad and I walking through this neighborhood, following a guide book, pointing at the broken guttering, the Masonic symbols made out of wood.

Damen next stop.

Doors open on the left at Damen.

Thank you for riding the blue line.

Mr Watson, Old Mrs Morse's father, had been a pal of one of the architects. All the houses have black roofs, so dark they soak in the sun, like the watertowers you see downtown. They've never made sense to me. I ask my dad and he says, 'Beats me why they make 'em black.'

'A witch's roof,' Mrs Morse says with a toothy grin. Her witch's roof and turret and the windows which curve round the southwest 'corner' of the house. Its truest, simple form facing the lake, its grandiose façade revealed to the neighborhood where appearances matter.

Old Mrs Morse stands in her front yard, looking at the elaborate designs of the front of her house, spade in hand, wet rich dirt wiped on her left thigh. 'My da, he knew how to play the game. He learned that fast. Before this place,' her spade swinging in a dismissive arc towards the new-built monstrosities, 'was the den of iniquity it is now.'

Mrs Morse is convinced her house will be knocked down by the Village, and eventually the land will end up in the hands of some young couple with more money than sense (more money than her), and no taste, who will build some en-suite infested box house which will hike property prices up even more. 'Who needs an uncouth old lady with a run-down, old-fashioned house?' It's a rhetorical question, but I answer her anyway.

'Me. I need this old lady.'

'Help me with this rose bush,' she says, tossing me the extra pair of gloves that have been hanging over her waistband.

'Sure thing Mrs Morse.'

'That's Ma'am to you.'

'Sure thing Ma'am.'

More clearly than last time I was on this street, I see all the parts that Mr Watson stole for his own house. A gargoyle here, a turret there, expensive curved windows in the place of corners. A dreamer, and his house testifies to it.

Eventually I get back to the Flat Iron Building and cross however many streets to get onto North Avenue and I head east, towards the lake.

A cut of air curls down my neck, so cold the air's almost solid. It's there, somewhere, no matter how I wrap the scarf. No one else is out walking. With good reason. Doesn't matter how you dress. No one can dress for this.

I don't really know the city all that well and, although I have a pocket map, I don't pull it out and look at it. I'd look like a foolish tourist. Which I'm not. This is my town. I walk. I'm sure that North Ave runs all the way east. The Chicago grid. Which I could learn if I spent even a day dedicating myself to understanding it. But I haven't. I'm bound to run into an 'El' stop.

But somewhere I'm not sure and a slight panic flutters low between my legs, from my stomach down to that point, inside, a flutter, a buzz, and it grows out to my fingers. I breathe slow and deep. Take note of street signs and directions, and I breathe in again, conscious of holding onto this feeling. This is my town. My kinda town and I'll find my way eventually.

Walking and thinking and crying. No one knows me. I am constantly walking through places, displacing perfection and, as I leave, allowing it to sweep back into place.

Past some sex shops, don't look, don't look. Over a bridge, isolated because it's an isolated place, not because no one else is walking on a bitter day like this, which is also true, a cement bridge over I-94, The Kennedy Expressway. And then things shift, get rich. Crisp banners hang from light poles. Lincoln Park. A neighborhood. In an outdoor shop, I buy a new headlight lamp and a new flashlight. I'm sure dad has WD40 at home. In the store's bathroom I consult my map. There's a subway stop near here, the Red Line. North and Clybourn.

I walk for ages around and around trying to find the damn thing. And when I finally realize it's this short squat building bang in the middle of everything I feel just plain stupid. So obvious. It's a great old building. Shiny white tiles.

Should I go north or south?

Although I'm tempted to go downtown; where I really want to go is Navy Pier. The forbidden zone. The most visited place in Chicago except by me. Even though I've badgered him again and again, Dad won't take me there.

'It's a cash trap,' he says. 'A cash guzzling nightmare.'

It's where I want to go now, problem is there's no stop on the 'El' for Navy Pier. I'd have to walk for miles or find the right bus. I can't be bothered with all that hassle.

Even though he won't take me there, Dad taunts me with his story of Dime Pier anyway. How when he was in his late teens he and Steve would go down to the shore and how there used to be a different pier, further out into the water, to the north or the south side, I can't remember which. This pier didn't go all the way into the shore.

'And so we'd get a boat, a dime for the pair of us; you had to take a boat. Rowed by a guy like Charon over the river Hades. To another world where we'd be underage and yet we'd drink beer and whisky and eat burgers and brats.' That's his youth. I sometimes wonder what my dime pier will be. If the last couple days are it, I'm totally screwed.

The train is hot, full of bodies. We emerge from the dark into the light. This isn't an express train, it's the Red Line and we'll make every stop.

Dadadadada, the sound movement, the sound in his blood. The rattle of wheels on a track, a stitched up scar. This city. The whistle of the air through a not quite sealed window at the front of the train. The roar of the movement, the buzz of the electricity through the tracks. Dad's not seeking out a thing, not a thing, but a journey. A feeling. This feeling but not this city, my city with its gothic steel black tracks, criss-crossed supports. Could he have planned his escape? His bag filled not with keys but with cash carefully saved up over the years. A false passport to take him across an ocean. And then he's on a different train, level tracks, racing through desolate countryside. The keys make noise in his pocket as he worries them. His fellow train travelers glare and he ignores them.

He tries to focus. There's a door he wants to return to, when he's finished this thing.

Around him land slips by, unlike any land he knows. It's not what he expects. It doesn't crowd in like the buildings at Fullerton, does not crowd parts of him out. Stags push their antlers into the purple black blue sky. He watches as the sky loses the blue and turns to slate, ebony.

When he gets off the train the air is cold and damp. But not bitter. There's a single building in the middle of this nowhere. Mountains sleeping all around him. The lights of the pub shine orange like in the movies. He orders a scotch and a room.

In the morning the giants are covered in snow; a nose, an arm, a hand exposed. A pregnant belly, a navel, an outie, black against the snow. Pools of tears at the bottom disguise themselves as lochs.

A small white bird. Its camouflage. Spring a long way off.

After a long walk, my dad is in a small wooden hut, a bothy, and it's high up, at the mouth of a river just before the water falls down the mountain.

And the night rises. Day falls. Rises and falls.

Sways back and forth.

Click-click, a bird calls.

A small trail slightly dark against the snow, in the falling light.

A crack.

I break open. My cheek near frozen to the window, my face split by shadow and light. The train moving beneath me.

Fullerton is next.

Doors open on the left at Fullerton.

Smoking, littering, and playing radios or loud devices is prohibited.

A woman with her book covered like a school book in plain brown paper. I wonder what she's hiding. Dumbing down or smarting up? We're being held up and then, finally, we move.

The houses so close on both sides. We pass by real slow. On the east side there's a smoldering, blackened wooden frame of the house. Shiny black blue with windows and furniture melted by fire.

Thank you for riding the CTA Red Line.

Soliciting on CTA trains is prohibited. Violators will be arrested.

A spark from a repair crew working on the tracks has caused it. The houses, so close. The sharp smell of smoke. I've been working on the railway, all my livelong days. I've been working on the railway, just to pass the time away.

Belmont is next. Doors open on the right at Belmont.

Saturday brunch at Ann Sather's. Cinnamon buns. My dad tells me not to lick my fingers. How can you not lick your fingers? Scoop up the white sugar frosting with your index finger and stick it in your mouth, lick your lips. How can you not?

Addison, doors open on the left at Addison.

He isn't what he professes to be. People rarely are. He professes to be here for me. He went to a lot of trouble to procure me, to keep me, or so he says. And now he's on a journey away from this city, this Gotham-like, fantasy city full of crime and poverty and absurd wealth. These sleek buildings, these twenty-three bridges. This corrupt past. This incredibly possible future.

Wrigley Field is empty, no flags flying, no bustle. No hope or disappointment. Just a shell.

Priority seating is intended for the elderly and disabled passengers. Your co-operation is requested.

Standing passengers please do not lean against the doors.

Sheridan is next. Doors open on the left at Sheridan.

Please familiarize yourself with the train's communications, posted in each carriage.

This is Sheridan.

Doors closing.

My dad in movement. His graceful walk; his run, silly as a clown's. He looks as silly when he swims as when he runs. My dad the giraffe, me a deer. He often exaggerates his awkwardness, his pole vault legs hilarious. He doesn't flail on land or water, at normal speed, no, he just unfolds himself and folds himself with each step, stretches to full length and he has grace; at full speed, he is absurd. On the train he moves with the speed.

I'm younger and we're visiting Duncan and Mel and we all go out on the small lake they've built their house beside. We go out in all seasons:

pontooning around small islands of reeds, water skiing and wiping out. Ice skating, wiping out.

My dad's long legs shunted onto a stretch of skis. He never finds the rhythm quickly, but he gets there eventually, pulling from low in the water to standing and then up and over the wake and back the hard way and over the other side of the wake.

And him and Duncan at the back of the boat, shouting encouragement to me. Mel driving, and turning around to see how I'm doing. Speeding up and slowing down each time I go down.

Then we go back to their house and cook Mel's homemade venison sausages and burgers on the grill. Her garden green and bursting, bursting. The wood of the house, warm, the floors hot with the sun. A crazy cat chasing a crazy dog sliding across the floor of the basement.

Telephone wires swoop along the sides of the tracks.

Granville is next.

Doors open at the left at Granville.

Welcome to Red Line run 402.

Soliciting on CTA is prohibited. Violators will be prosecuted.

'At Granville, just one block west (away from the lake) and north (back towards home) is an Ethiopian restaurant. I took your mom there. Linden babysat.' His voice is intimate. Telling me something I shouldn't really know. 'It was a fiasco.'

He cranes his neck back to see the sign but it's gone. 'You can't see it from the train.'

At the next stop he talks about a bar where he and Steve stay late drinking, and how more than once Steve gets into a brawl. That one fight takes three days to make right, he tells me.

I see it clearly now. How Mel often pops in too. A few days into one of Linden's stays. Like it's spontaneous, generous. Like she wants to see me and Dad. She's always surprised he's not in. The two-hour trip from Wisconsin. Mel and her veggies in a canvas bag (no to plastic, down with plastic), with fresh organic meat, beef or venison. I always imagine she wrestles the field-fattened cow to the ground herself. Wields the knife. Knows how to do things, real things, practical things. She uses milk from local dairies. Not the industrial ones advertised by huge plastic cows with heads that move and moo. Not the ones dad moos back to every time we go up there to visit Duncan and Mel.

She doesn't go to those dairies with deep fried cheese sticks and milkshakes so thick the spoon stands up and doesn't sink. Instead, she buys her eggs from the small organic farmer with a hand-painted sign advertising homemade cheese and beer.

'We're part of something bigger,' Mel says. 'Even if it looks like we're alone and small. Time slows down for us, it becomes bigger and we can step into it, make it matter. Make things last.'

Linden stays for dinner, her and Mel talking long into the night. Long after I go to bed. Mel saying she's glad she'd put an overnight bag in the car, just in case. Linden's gone the next day and Mel often stays for days, and after dinner most nights the two of us go and garden, usually at Mrs Morse's, by the light of the moon, or my dad's old kerosene lamp. Mrs Morse invites us in for cookies and milk and she and Mel talk for ages, herb this and vegetable that and global change whatever. Sometimes I go home without Mel and sneak a glass of chocolate milk, more cookies, and read in bed, with a flashlight when I hear Mel come back.

Howard is next. As far as this train goes.

Transfer to the Purple and Yellow Line trains at Howard.

All change at Howard.

Birds of prey again. On the freezing platform. The pigeons too cold to care. Some with only one foot, a stump for the other. Like a candle nub.

Dingdong. The bells before the doors.

The egg timer Mel sets for the rice. 'It's the seasalt,' Mel says as she cooks another of her elaborate meals with all the best ingredients, which I try hard to love but often walk away thinking, what's so wrong with eating the same stuff over and over again?

'Diversity equals stability,' Mel says. She doesn't quote the stats any more: ninety-five per cent of diverse species killed by mass farming, the western habits that demand conformity to the lowest common denominator. I know this stuff now. I used to listen. But now that dad's gone, I think, what's so wrong with stability, reliability? With waking up and knowing exactly what you're going to get?

Why does it matter?

Once it's gone, it's gone.

Until it comes back.

This is Howard.

Doors closing.

Welcome to Purple Line run 512.

South Boulevard is next.

Doors open at the left at South Boulevard.

All the telephone poles at an angle, pushed away from the train, wires slack, ready to be snapped. Linden texts to say to meet her at dad's shop in an hour. We need to check that it's okay. See if he's left behind any clues. I know what we'll find.

Nothing. A big fat nothing.

Any good parent will tell you there are things they don't tell their kids.

This puts me at a disadvantage. All this stuff I don't know. What he's left behind is in too much of a mess to make sense of. How he's done this before. Lots of times before.

Main is next.

Doors open at the right at Main.

This is Main.

Doors closing.

The main drag. The coffee shop where Mel and Duncan first meet when they're freshmen at Northwestern. The coffee shop with its white ceramic mugs and huge slices of homemade cake. Duncan's total belief in himself; Mel, tanned and young, like she's just been plucked from the earth, beautiful. How can she not win his heart? How does he win hers?

Dempster is next.

Doors open at the right at Dempster.

Standing passengers please do not lean against the doors.

The first hints of a wisdom tooth. But I'm not any wiser.

Sometimes I imagine my mom's not dead at all but that dad simply told me that to stop all my questions.

'Where is my mom?'

'She's far away,' he says, 'really far away.'

'When will we go there?'

'We will, Roe. But not just yet.'

'Why not? I want to see her.'

'We'll both get there eventually,' he says.

Stroking his chin where his beard used to be. True or absolutely misleading, his stories which are designed to make me love him more. To wipe out all the doubt about his love.

This is Dempster.

Doors closing.

Davis is next.

Doors open at the right at Davis.

Right on Davis!

His classmates mock him in gym class where he scissors along the muddy field kicking up clumps and getting splattered as people pass him by.

Gym teachers berate him. 'If we could sort your stride, improve your lungs, you'd be the perfect marathoner.' But he can imagine nothing worse. Running sets his teeth on edge, like his bones are connected by rubber bands, boing boing boing.

Foster is next.

Doors open at the right at Foster.

Soliciting is prohibited…

This is Foster.

Doors closing.

Smoking…

Rolling roll-ups under the bleachers. Pretty things beside him. What's his poison? Bourbon? Vodka? Tequila? Is he a smooth talker? Do his eyes betray his desire? Under the bleachers smoking and drinking and kissing. And getting ready to flee.

This is Noyes.

Doors closing.

Central is next.

Doors open at the left at Central.

Purple roof at Central.

He's determined to go. I know that. He's so at ease as we sit there. His hands move just as they always do, his smile just as easy. His hug no longer or shorter than usual. He feels as strong and steady as always. I love you Roe, my foundling. And I believe him. And somehow I just know that he doesn't love me as much as he loves this key, because there's no mystery left about me.

He just needs some time, to come back to his senses. To me. That's why I take the slow train.

Linden is next.

First comes Duncan, the straight arrow, thinking his way is the only right way. That he deserves the world. Then Peter, the troublemaker, thinking the world owes him nothing, but that he'll take what he needs. And Linden is next, the youngest by far, picking up the pieces. And the Davis family train just rides and rides and rides and makes all the stops.

The El is nearly empty. Two other people in the carriage with me. Both older women. Both in furs. Before Linden we pass over a small, beautiful bridge. One of the only level crossings of the journey. The second is at Maple. The barriers come down but there's no sound as we pass.

This is Linden. As far as this train goes. All passengers must leave the train.
Thank you for riding the CTA Purple Line.
Doors closing.

Beyond our house the water is the color of teeth, trees the color of cement. And the Village has put up a new sign between our houses:

Submerged Rocks
Inclement weather dangers ahead.
Proceed at your own risk.

The answering machine blinks, winks. The school has called about my unexplained absence and my F minus. Somewhere my dad's phone has rung and taken the same message. A policeman has phoned, with a gruff manner, a cold-creaking voice, and he says they have nothing new. I erase them both.

I flip the shop keys off the hook. They are butterflies in my hand. The flashlight is heavy against my thigh. Mrs Morse's keys rattling around my bag.

I take the long way around so I don't pass Carl's. My dad's shop is narrow with a good window at the front. Stuffed between the shoe shop on the corner and a bakery that used to be a florist that was a laundry before that and supposedly, originally, a pharmacy.

'What was your shop before?' I ask my dad.

'Wasted space.'

'What?'

'Storage space for whatever. When I bought it, first thing I had to do was shift all the junk people had hoarded in here over the years. It's really just another room to Joe's bit next door. They didn't need it. Thought they'd make some money out of it.' He knocks on the wall with an open hand. Hollow.

'Will you stop doing that?' yells Joseph Cardonald, the baker. 'I know it's shoddy. One of these days you'll put up half the money and build a proper wall!'

But dad likes listening to the hustle and bustle of next door. The domestic squabbles between Joe and his son.

The keys slide smoothly. Of course. The window is filthy. The handle well used. Inside I should notice things but all I know is how familiar it all is. Suddenly Linden is behind me, a hand on my shoulder. She gives it a small squeeze and walks past me, careful not to disturb anything.

How would it look if he was coming back tomorrow?

How would it look if he meant to be away for a long time?

Exactly like this. Exactly like this.

The counters are end of the day clear. Neat sets of keys, with tags, waiting to be collected. Envelopes for the single keys. Scrawled names. The smell of metal. The industry, the beauty of the machines. I run my hand over a mitre. Linden doesn't stop me. It's clear that this is a shop of someone who means to come back. It's crystal clear.

My dad's handwriting is barely legible. Only after years of immersion can I make out most of the letters. The other bits we will have to interpret through blind luck.

'There are things in this life I will dedicate time to. Making my handwriting neat is not one of those things,' he says.

'It'd be helpful if I could read your notes.'

'You do just fine. I make my numbers clear.'

Clearish, I think.

Mrs Robert's keys taped to two new locks. Waiting for my dad to install them. She's a regular. I saw her son around just last week, home for his usual punch and grab until she kicks him out and changes the locks. She'll be needing these keys. Dad doesn't charge her any more since the black eye, the ring of bruises around her wrists. She feigns gardening accidents, a clumsy mis-step, but doesn't look at him. I pocket her keys and the new locks.

The answer phone blinks and blinks and blinks.

'We should put a sign up,' Linden says. 'Let people know he'll be back.'

'We should open the shop up on Saturday or something. So people can pick up their keys.'

'This place looks…' she starts, doesn't finish.

'Like he either intended to come back or he wanted to make it appear like he was going to.'

Linden writes a sign about the Saturday opening.

'Ten to twelve?'

'Make it nine to twelve, people like to get up and out early round these parts.'

'These parts?'

'You know, the fast-paced suburbs.'

The sign's up. The news will be out tomorrow anyway. Tomorrow will be different shit, same fan.

I grab my dad's tool box on the way out. 'Can you swing by Laurel Circle?'

Mrs Robert's house is solid, a newer house, a fortress of bricks, impenetrable at ground level. Her only weakness is her thieving son.

Linden drops me off. 'I'll see you at home.'

Her bell is an old-fashioned, ceramic circle that you pull out to ring. A crescent moon, lit up from behind. Something salvaged from a previous house? It's such a great bell, I pull it twice.

Her face is prepared for battle when she comes to the door, and then it relaxes when she sees me. 'Oh, hello Roe. I thought you were kids tampering with my bell. Since it glows it seems to attract the ding dong ditch crowd.'

'It's fabulous, I couldn't resist a second pull.'

'A gift from my antique-hunting dead husband. Alive, of course, when he gave it to me.' She smiles, her face is free of hassle, as far as I can tell. 'What can I do for you Roe?'

'I'm here to change your locks.'

She looks behind me. 'Where's Peter?'

'He's away this week and asked me to do it for him.'

'He was supposed to do it on Saturday.'

'I know. It's been one of those weeks.'

'Do you know what you're doing?'

'I'm not an expert like dad, but they'll be solid when I'm done.'

The screwdriver bites into the wood, the lock pops out and I pop another in. It's the same for the back door. My knitted gloves get in the way and I have to do it bare-fingered. My hands are red and stiff when I'm done. I hand her the new keys.

'Come in and warm up.'

'Thanks, but I need to be getting home.'

'Give your father my best.'

'I will. You take care of yourself.'

She knows exactly how to do that.

Even the back stairs are shovelled and salted. The ground cover is getting old and crunchy and dirty. It's fast terrain now but even so, by the time I get home it's dark. There are boys already down at the beach. Bragging. The air is cold and their voices meet no resistance.

I go to Mrs Morse's. There's thick frost on the windows. When I scratch at them, I can't see in. It's only been a year since they took her away. Between Christmas and New Year. She was dead by the fireworks. I still think the Village killed her. Dad's more philosophical.

'Maybe it allowed her to let go.'

'What if she didn't want to let go?'

'Roe, she lived a good, long life.'

'Not long enough.'

He kisses my forehead. 'It has to be long enough, Roe. We can't do anything to change it now.'

I scrunch my face. Almost stomp my foot like a child. He brings it out in me sometimes. This blind, grumpy stubbornness. It's too much him here, him too smart, smug. Know-it-all. Always a placating word. How annoying. Living with someone who is right all the time.

There is a right and a wrong way. I'm sure of it.

He gets a lawyer to protect her house. And other than that I have no idea who he is to Mrs Morse.

The door stands in the middle of the living room floor. It's sanded and clean. I find WD40 in my dad's toolbox, oil the hinges, and when I turn the handle it arcs open easily. I step through. It used to be magic, I'd feel the tingle of all these unknown things, unknown possible worlds. Now it's just a door, is a door, is a door.

I step through again. And again. And I close the door behind me.

My dad doesn't forbid me from going upstairs, from entering Mrs Morse's bedroom. Not exactly. It's not so much how he stands at the top of the stairs, but the very fact that he does, much of the time. So it's not that I can't go up there, it's just that I don't go up there. By the end, when I'm spending some nights at her house, looking after her, she's on the sofabed downstairs, the stairs are too much for her to take.

In her bedroom the bed's been pulled away from the wall at a slight angle. Pulled with one hand, hooked underneath. It has that feeling. It faces the window, within a long arm's reach of the pictures.

Pictures of a young woman and my dad. And Mrs Morse. They are radiant. They are everything to each other and nothing. It's summer. My dad and the girl look sixteen or so and there's nothing as big as they are.

No one's ever mentioned a girl to me.

The girl.

My dad is holding her hand. His body, from the hips down, pulls towards her like it's being pulled sideways by gravity. She's the earth. His upper half turns towards the sun, a sway away, to the west. I know it's the west.

And he's caught between.

Mrs Morse captures the moment of his indecision, in the midst of his exuberance. His black curls, him waving at the camera, waving goodbye? How must Mrs Morse feel? This boy, this lovely boy, who has this girl's heart, her daughter? I feel sure of it, sure that this beautiful girl is Mrs Morse's daughter. And her heart is my dad's, and he's a stilt-legged bird, about to take flight.

My dad with the wind at his heels.

Why have I never seen this before? Never noticed it before? I see it here because it's so obvious, it's the look he holds when his guard is down.

How blind have I been?

The answers are always closer to home than you think. Always the simplest. I bet if I dusted for fingerprints I know whose prints I'd find.

Mrs Morse's house is in the background. A tea party. Her old iron table, wrought with thick flowers and waxy leaves, painted an intolerable white. An old-fashioned iron holds down the tablecloth. The girl's hand is on one side. Towards the lake, blue lapping between her fingers. Her right hand is clutched comfortably by my dad. His red cheeks. Her brown, wild curls, bleached with the sun, her skin, her face, all of her aglow.

I think, girlfriend, senior prom date. She's a pretty girl; why the hell has no one ever told me about her? It's obvious she's important to him and to Mrs Morse. A picture to capture that feeling. The laughter of the afternoon. In the smallest imagined movement of the trees, small white tops to the waves on the beach. The lake high, you can see it. Licking close to the top. And the three of them oblivious. It won't take the house until the winter storms. It will all be different then.

I turn the picture over. Slide the back off. It's buckled. Moldy at the edges, there'll be names on the back with a date. Of course there will. Always are in the movies.

But the picture is crumpled and unmarked. Who has to put the names on the back of their most cherished photographs? Who has to name the people most important to them?

Mrs Morse is family. She and my dad are always planning, conspiring, to fix this or that. And often they talk long into the night and I fall asleep with my head in her lap, or his. This back and forth. This bond, and never once do I question what brings them together. Never once do I imagine it's a girl.

The foolish ignorance of the young. Shit. I'm so young and so ignorant. How have I survived this long?

'Isn't it cool,' Linden says, beer in hand, 'that in baseball, tension replaces action?'

She's got in the tape of 'that game'. Well, the most recent fiasco of a game. I've got the photos in my square jacket pocket. I don't know why Linden always does this, re-watches the worst games of past seasons. It always upsets her, makes her pine for a world that doesn't yet exist—a world where the Cubs actually believe in themselves, a world that exists whole and complete before that moment is irrevocably lost.

'What are you talking about?' I shake off my coat, pull my hat off and my hair is instant static, I shrug off one boot and then the other. I hang my coat over the back of the kitchen chair. 'Isn't the perfect game when we win?'

'Philistine. We're talking baseball theory here. Play along.' She winks and grins at her own, saddo, humor. 'In a perfect game,' she repeats, 'in a no-hitter, it's like we're all just sitting here waiting, waiting, tense, wanting our team to be the one to break that inaction with a hit.'

'Preferably our team, with a home run.' I say.

'We're waiting for *something*,' she repeats.

'Couldn't you look at it as tension as an active state itself? With two forces in opposition and then one pulls too hard or the other lets go or tugs hard, breaks that tautness. Action. A win.'

Linden stares at me. 'When did you get so smart?'

'I'm not smart.'

'Sounds like it to me.'

Her eyes fix on the screen. The scene is the opposite of tense, it's a free-for-all. That ball, the poor man's interference. That fated moment.

She presses rewind, and the ball goes back, a perfect chance, again, possible. And the next second, impossible.

She pauses it, the ball fumbles in the air. The stupid Cubs fan barely catches the thing.

I grin. 'So, is stillness just a pause between one activity and another? Or an end in and of itself? Or is movement simply activity bookended by the stillness of a beginning and an end?'

'Shit.' She rubs her head. 'What sort of drugs are you on?'

'Our teacher has been talking about stuff like this all week.'

'Philosophy?'

'Communications. Most people are fed up.'

'And you?'

'I've not decided yet. I'm mulching.'

'I think we start with stillness and will return to stillness.'

'What about activity that no one witnesses? A silence or stillness or non-action that's assumed?'

'If a tree falls in the woods and no one hears it, has it fallen?'

When in doubt fall back on a cliché. 'Kind of,' I say. 'Sound and light don't displace anything. But they still act upon us, affect us.'

'The sound of the ball on the bat, the roar of the crowd.'

'Exactly. They affect us emotionally but don't change anything physically.'

'What about the sound barrier? The boom?'

'Do we feel it?' I ask.

'Yes, in our bodies, our ears.'

'Yeah, I don't know. I'm sort of thinking about emotions too.'

'Which ones?'

'Hope and despair. Faith and belief. Joy and anger. Love and solitude.'

'Emotions?'

I don't continue. I break off. Action displacing tension.

'Was there ever a girl?' I ask.

'What?'

'For dad. One that was a reason rather than an excuse?'

'No, Roe. Your dad's one of the world's greatest bachelors. A few have wanted to be his girl but none ever succeed.'

I don't believe her. There's me and before me there was her. I'm sure of it. 'When did Mr Morse die?'

'A long time ago. I was six or seven.'

When dad was seventeen.

'How?'

She says nothing. She pauses the video. 'Fess up Roe, what have you found?'

'A photograph, at Mrs Morse's.'

I slide it out of my coat pocket, hand it to Linden. It's like handing over a sliver of ice.

'She was beautiful,' Linden says.

'Who?'

'Lauren.'

'Lauren Morse,' I offer.

Linden's eyes look up, she's not surprised I know. 'Yes. The love of many people's lives.'

'And…'

'And she died. She and her dad were on their way back from visiting his family in Alabama.' She pauses, time running a line in her head. 'The winter of Peter's senior year. I think they were coming back early because the lake had taken the house. I'm not sure. Anyway they took the train because he didn't like to fly, and it derailed into a river.'

'And.'

'And Mr Morse died on the spot, Lauren was thrown clear and drowned. It was devastating. Peter left right after. Fled. Didn't even wait until graduation.'

So, no high school diploma for my dad.

'He didn't come back again until Grandpa got ill.'

'And.'

'And what else do you want to know?'

What does it mean? Did he love her? Did losing her make him restless? Did it eventually tie him to this place and Mrs Morse and me? Did his love for her affect his decision to take me in?

'Why doesn't anyone ever talk about her?'

She rubs her face with an open palm. Takes a few breaths. 'Good question. I'm not sure. Maybe it's too hard. Too raw. Caused so many problems.'

'Come on Linden, stop avoiding.'

'I'm not, Roe. It's not black and white. It's not that simple. The lake was so high. Mrs Morse was alone. We were all just scared. My mom and Peter spent a lot of time helping Mrs Morse move things to the second floor and to the western half of the house. That week turned crazy. The lake, the house, Lauren, Mr Morse. I think back and Mrs Morse must have been young, in her early forties or something. That's the week that turned her older.'

But that's not the reason. 'People talk about the house, the lake, and I knew that Mr Morse existed and had died. Why not Lauren?'

'I don't know Roe. I can't answer that.'

'You said problems. What problems?'

'It's not like her death caused them but… Peter left, our mom died soon after. Dad seemed fine, but he got old fast, although it was years before the cancer took hold. And Peter was just off the map for years and years. It took him and Mrs Morse a long time to get to talking again.'

'Why?'

'Come on, Roe, give me a break. This is stuff you should talk with your dad about.'

'Great theory. You see him here? You hear him talking?'

Linden doesn't even look around. Here and now we know it's just the two of us. I continue for her. 'So he'd dropped Lauren like a hot potato. The train trip was a treat her parents gave her to help her stop thinking about Peter. Or was she preggos at the time and I'm their love child and he took me away originally and Mrs Morse got pissed off because she's my grandmother and didn't get to see enough of me?'

This last bit is absurd, the timeline is all wrong, I'm out by at least ten years, but I say it anyway. Linden smiles. 'Are you applying this imagination in school?'

'All the time.'

'Lauren was just a girl. A beautiful girl who everyone loved and who died. That's it. It's just too much. Too much, Roe. It's sensible not to talk about it.'

'And my mom?'

She lowers her eyes. Wipes her eye with the sleeve of her upper arm. Not a tell of a lie, but of emotion.

'Another beautiful girl. A lost girl. Not so simple.'

I raise an eyebrow. 'Go on, spit it out. And not just the story my dad's so fond of.' Mr R might think the truth is too complicated to talk about. But who can be bothered with the cloak and dagger stuff.

'Peter tells a good story,' Linden says.

'But it's not true.'

I expect her to contradict me. But she doesn't. My breastbone breaks in half. A sharp intake of breath. I cough to cover it.

What is the truth? A lie removed and pureness restored? Or something additional, an imposition. Something you need to get over? Get used to?

What don't I know?

'Your mother, Chris, was a rock climber. Peter and her had run into each other once or twice out west. When it comes down to it I think all she wanted to do was climb, and have sex with ranch hands. She was really good at it from what Peter says.'

'The climbing or the sex?'

'Ha ha,' Linden says.

'Were they ever a couple?'

'They might have met up under the stars once or twice.'

Is that an answer or a swerve? 'Linden, answer the question.'

'As Peter tells it, she got pregnant by some cowboy who drank too much and was fond of swinging a gun around when drinking tequila, and once too often he pointed it in her direction. She was house-sitting in the area and ran into Peter when she got locked out one day. She had no idea he was a locksmith.'

As Peter tells it. How would my mom tell it?

'Why was she here?'

'I don't know.'

'So she just happened to go into dad's shop?'

Linden raises an eyebrow. 'Nail on the head.'

'He always says her walking into the shop was just random.'

Linden fidgets. The hand. The extra breath.

'I don't know Roe. It could have been.' But it's not. Everything about Linden's voice says she thinks it's otherwise. 'Your mom was beautiful and Peter was lonely. He brought her home. She stayed for a week or two. When the climbing bug took hold again, she left you with Peter.'

So easy. To leave her daughter in the hands of a stranger.

'He didn't know her well enough for her to do that. But she did anyway. He didn't know what to do. He didn't know. He was lost. Upset. Dad, grandpa, only had a few months to live. Your mom had stumbled into a house filled with death, and love, and it was better than where she'd come from. But Peter didn't love her. Couldn't.'

'He still loved Lauren.'

Linden gets up. Rubs one socked foot on the other. Goes to the window and looks at Mrs Morse's house. Beyond, to the sky and the lake.

'You really should be talking to your dad about this.'

'But I'm not. I'm talking to you.'

Spit it out. Whatever it is.

'She didn't just leave you the one time and never came back. She'd return for a few weeks, fight with Peter, with herself, and then leave again.'

Always being left. There's a history of it. But this is nothing I didn't know about my mom. She loved me, she left me. It was for the best.

But Linden's not finished.

'One time she went off and got herself killed. A rock climbing accident. She fell four hundred feet. You were only two years old. She'd given him custody in her will.'

My mom dead. Dead as a doorknob. Dead as dead.

'So it's true then. She's really dead.'

Linden sits down. Peers.

'Didn't Peter tell you that?'

'Yeah. I just thought he said it to make me feel protected. To make me love him more, because he was all I had.'

There's just me and him. Him and me. That's the way it's always going to be.

'So he didn't have a choice. He had to raise me.'

'It's not like that, Roe.'

'What is it like then?'

'He didn't have to keep you.'

'Who made him then? Who twisted his arm to keep me? You? Mel? Duncan? My mom?'

'It wasn't like that.'

'What was it like?'

'Your mom, Chris, was a beautiful girl too. Who kept making bad choices. She wanted Peter to leave with her. Wanted him to love her. But he

Elizabeth Reeder

couldn't. But he loved you and…'

'And?'

'Let's just say her and motherhood weren't always on speaking terms. She found the baby-crying thing difficult.'

I imagine it. My mom tearing her hair out. 'She never stops crying. She never fucking stops.' My hard little fists, my red face, wet with tears. Legs going crazy. Strong and rigid.

'You're the one making the noise,' my dad says to her.

Her hard look. The same as mine when I'm really angry. 'You're as maddening as her.' And how she swings her already packed rucksack over her back and slams the door.

'Don't babies drive lots of people mad?' I ask Linden.

'Yes, but she just had the sense to leave before she did some harm. Peter might have followed, with you, but Dad was still here, getting weaker every day, and that meant everything to him. Something worth staying for. And he was going to keep you here with him. I mean, he's never talked about it, but I also think him and Mrs Morse needed each other. I've almost thought that they…'

'Thought what?'

'Nothing. Nothing at all. They needed each other. He couldn't leave. Chris couldn't take care of you on her own. He wanted to keep you. Mrs Morse offered to help too.'

She rips off an uneven nail, chucks it over the back of the couch. Which is gross, but I do it too when no one is watching so I let it slide.

I'm a broken record, with a broken heart, with my ears pounding. Truth is something added, pushing out the space.

'So he didn't have a choice?'

She's picking her nails. I grab her left hand away and hold it between mine. To stop her from ripping her nails down too low.

'No, Roe, he didn't.' I look up. I knew it. Her feet flexing and pointing, stretching the muscles in her legs.

But she continues, 'It was love at first sight. He could do nothing but love you and keep you. You could argue he simplified the story because he wanted you always to know that he had a choice, and he chose you.'

I sink down.

And I want to believe her. That my mother loved me, and that's why she left me with a man she was infatuated with but could never have. And that my dad loves me, which is why he's left me too. I want to believe Linden. Really I do.

Before I can speak, I'm saved by the doorbell.

'I'll get it,' I say and I'm already up and over the back of the couch. Quiz will be standing there, like I've willed it.

Quiz is a rugby player, which boggles my mind. I have no idea what he does out there on the field. Group hugs, scrums, ballet-like leaps to fight for the possession of the ball, shoving the ball between your legs for some sort of homoerotic hand-off. Far more violent than football, or baseball where most injuries are self-inflicted. I should care, I know this. I go to the games. Yell with the crowd. Hug and kiss him even when he's covered in sweat and grime and far worse things like blood and snot and sick.

The first time my dad meets Quiz, he comes over after a rugby game, one of the last ones last season. And although he's cleaned himself up a bit, he can't hide the bust-up lip, the gash above his eye, and yet he's still managed to get all his brow piercings back in. I wince at the thought. His black hair flashes red at the tips in the sun, his scrunch-dyed bright blue shirt clings to his chest and his arms, hangs looser across his stomach. His big bag jeans have thin cable cord running down the sides and along the bottom. They are a slightly brighter blue than regular denim. Color. He's pure color and my dad can barely bring himself to shake his hand. He has this look on his face that I will become more used to. Horror? Dismay? Fear?

Fear. Because it isn't just the way he looks at Quiz, and asks, 'And your real name is?' It's the way he looks back at me, searching my face for some recognition of the absurdity of this.

'It's short for Quizzical, if that's any help Mr Davis.' And I see it in Quiz, mirrored in my dad. His one eyebrow rises naturally in an expression of curiosity, in questioning. 'My parents say it's the way I looked.'

'It's the eyebrows,' I add, 'they've always looked a bit devilish.'

This is said with a grin. And my dad shoves his shoulders down. Oops. Far too intimate on my part. Quiz picks up my slack.

'My dad's a mathematician too, so it suited his empirical testing of knowledge.'

'And your mom liked the fact that her kid had a "z" in his name.'

'Yeah, that too.'

'There's always Zach,' my dad says, unhelpfully, not quite joking.

But he's my own skater boy. I know it's a bit out of style. That's me all over. Slightly out of style. I'd like coolness to come easily, wouldn't we all? Or attitude or genius or anything that is the right shape for the right peg.

And so it's Wednesday and my dad's been gone for one hundred and twenty hours. Approximately.

Quiz comes to the door. Rings the bell even though I've left it unlocked. The boy has manners. I find I like manners.

Quiz is here. Filling up the doorway, with his oh-so-solid body. The very meat of him. All right there, time won't get him. You can see it. He'll move from young to old and be the eighty-year-old you see in jeans, young in body, wise in face. The hair will be its natural grey, he'll have given up the slight punk skater image. He'll never wear a suit. His smile will always take over his face, transforming simple beauty to comedy. My beautiful comedian.

The offhand voice, scratchy, of the policeman nags behind my ear. The lack of my dad's smell hits me too. Already the house smells more female. I pull Quiz inside. He grins. I am won over. My tenacity, my fear runs down my body, buries itself deeper. He doesn't need to know these things yet. My dad is just missing. I keep looking back towards my dad and seeing it there—fear in his eyes when he first meets Quiz. This infant now a girl, almost a woman. With a mouth on her and a boyfriend with blue hair and dark eyes that look at her in a way no father wants his daughter to be looked at.

Now I'd give anything to have my dad here and to tell Quiz to go home. But dad's not here and Quiz stays through dinner and when we're tired we go to bed. We move slowly. My muscles are stretched and locked and released. Exhausted from the long walk.

It is here that time is pressed into the very thinnest fabric of fact. Where his breath is slow and fast and slow again. When the glide and stretch of him means nothing else matters. He weaves a web, ethereal and yet almost strong enough to keep me there, for a short while. When I sleep he pulls my arm over him, my leg. Holding me in place as if he already knows I'm too much for him. That I know I'm too much for him.

We wake up to dark surfaces, darker shadows. Our breath thick and bound. The fact of him binds me down. How fast. Just three days ago it grounded me, made me more me. Now it makes me more his.

He slips downstairs and back home. Where his mother will be waiting for him. And she'll want to call Linden and yell, 'Do you know what your niece and my son are up to? You've got no right to make these choices for her that Peter wouldn't want her to make!' And yet she wants Quiz to know this feeling, of loving someone and sticking with them through a tough time. It will make him a better man. But he's not a man. He's a boy, her son. And she knows, and I know, he's not up to it.

With Quiz gone I sink into the dark. It's cool and clean and mine.

THURSDAY

'PMA,' Mrs Warner says, like she's leading some weirdo consciousness raising group from the seventies. 'Positive Mental Attitude.' Each word. Crisp and annoying. 'If you believe it will be okay, if you have a positive outlook, it will all be okay.'

No note, nothing. I couldn't bring myself to tell Linden. I've come to homeroom without a note. What do you do without a note?

'Roe, you know the rules.'

'I was thinking you'd be positive about the absence of a note.' She dismisses me simply by looking down at the roll call. And I take myself off to the Dean.

'So, it's you again Miss Davis.' Mrs Melbourne looks at me over her glasses, a pen twirling in her fingers.

I nod. Shrug my shoulders.

'I wasn't at school yesterday.'

'Let me guess. And you don't have a note.'

'Righty-oh.'

'Is there anything you want to tell me?'

'No.'

She raises an eyebrow.

'No, ma'am.'

'Are you sure?'

The corner of the *Glenlyon Life* is just visible on a chair by the window, where you can often see her sitting in the morning watching the students arrive.

The news is out. There's an army in my chest. A mallet tapping behind my ears.

'Any problems at home?'

As if she doesn't already know. The game's up.

'Yeah, my dad's missing.'

'That's pretty big, Roe.'

'I suppose.'

'How are you?'

How do I look? How am I acting? What do you think? How would you like it? 'He's just doing it to make a point.'

'What point?'

'How the hell should I know?'

She lets the swearing slide.

'Where were you yesterday?'

'Out and about.'

'You missed your history test.'

She doesn't miss a beat.

'That was sort of part of the plan.'

'Roe, this must be really hard for you.' I keep my head down. My shoes are a mess, crusted with road salt. 'But you need to keep communicating with people. Try not to take it all on yourself. Let us know what you need. You don't have to deal with this by yourself.'

But I do. No one else has been left. No one else can fill his shoes. Can they make him come back? Make him phone? Or send a postcard to let me know he's okay?

'I'd like to drop history. It doesn't make any sense. Pavich is a creep.'

'You need your parent's signature to do that. All forms have to be in by noon.'

I'm screwed.

'But I'll sign yours. As a temporary measure. And give you a note for homeroom, for history. But you've got to promise to come to school. You'll have to go to history, the class switch won't happen until Monday.'

'Thanks.'

In chemistry there's a student missing in action. Not a day too soon. Turns out Scott's set his garage on fire. Killed the family dog in the process. Singed his hands pretty badly. I wonder if the doctors had a dilemma: to hospitalize him because of his hands or his chemical pyromania?

I am without a lab partner. Which is a blessing.

Between classes the halls are packed. Jammed with well-wishers. Ambulance chasers. 'Are you okay? Roe?'

'I hear your dad's missing? Are you okay?'

'Where do you think he's gone? How do you feel? Are you okay?'

A soft rub on my upper arms, a tilted head. Concern. Knitted eyebrows and beady eyes storing up my dark circles, my clean line of lips. Gossip fodder.

'Are you okay?'

'Are you okay?'

I'll pound the next person.

But it's Cath and Caroline and they're great and silent. Just short hugs and snobby Abi says nothing but nods. And I remember that her mom had cancer and was away for a long time. Is she still alive? Shit, I should know that. I nod back.

Quiz's pals slap me on the shoulder.

'Your dad's a fool to leave you.'

'Thanks, John.'

'You should come to practice on Sunday. If you're looking for something to do.'

'Maybe,' I say.

All these bodies, crammed in, swooping in for a bit of me. And I don't see Jess or Quiz or anyone who'll treat me just the same as always. I give my locker a swerve and head right for Mr R's class. I'm the first one in and I sit in the back of the class, not in my assigned seat.

Each presence that disappears restores perfection. It's almost unbearable. Like school. All these words. Your dad. Your dad. Your dad. There and then gone. People file into class and find new spaces since I've disrupted the natural order.

Mr R sits at the front of the class not saying a thing. He glances around, never resting too long on me. It's a measured avoidance. I can tell. No one says a word.

'Let's experience silence,' he says. 'Let's see where it takes us.'

But he doesn't want silence, he wants time to think. To remember all the expostulations he's made all week.

The desk I'm sitting at has darkly drawn action heroes all over it. Bam, says one bubble. Shazam, says another. A heroine with huge tits says nothing.

I imagine Mrs R left the imperfection that was her marriage and her absence, in turn, has created peace, like the lack of wind after a storm, and that Mr R has been improving on the situation by removing pictures, happy pictures with the two of them standing, usually slightly off-center, in front of some geological majesty. He's filled big black bags with her clothes, make-up, silverware. The jewelry he places in a pretty box he finds on the floor of the closet and he'll hawk it, for cash, a tidy sum, later and buy himself… I don't think he'll buy himself anything right away, but the perfect object will make itself known, soon enough.

This morning Mr R has realized that his beloved disappeared around the same time as my dad, the local locksmith. He hadn't known this until Mr Crick, lazy layabout Crick, showed him the *Glenlyon Life* police report at a coffee break they share. The news all around school, hot, blustery, by mid-morning.

Roe Davis, he thinks, abandoned.

And I'd been in his class on Monday and Tuesday. He'd not noticed a thing different about me. His heart on his sleeve, mine beating rat a tat tat, like normal, in my chest. There was my unapproved absence yesterday. Was that perfection or did it take him, and the class, further away from what was right? Natural?

Mr R considers.

Further away, he concludes.

I hope.

He allows himself a quick glance in my direction. My dark hair and my so long, Roe long legs which have tripped him up once or twice, by accident, when he paces excitedly, unexpectedly at the front of the class.

Definitely further away from perfection.

And his theories are honing themselves into a fine pinpoint of pure light. Are we both considering the one possible, logical conclusion?

My dad and his wife. Together. The space they take up (hot, sweaty, smelling of sex) and how fast they move from place to place, how fast they must move, corrupting, displacing and as they move on, the space returns to normal, peaceful, true.

He claps his hands three times. Sharp and clear. The silence is broken.

'Don't just accept what I say. I'm throwing things out for you to consider. Don't take what other people say at face value either. Find your own truths. Read the signs.'

'A good way to do this is to figure out what your question is, then your answer will actually mean something.' Mr R looks like he's combed his hair today but his beard's a mess and I'm not sure he's made it all the way to doing the laundry. He's crumpled and I can smell him from the back row. Do I look this obviously lost?

'Like 42,' Missy says. A hitchhiker in her own universe.

'Exactly. Exactly.'

Shut up. Shut up. Shut up.

'Without the right questions, you have a combination padlock without numbers.'

'A door with no handle,' Missy offers.

'A car without a steering wheel,' adds Mr R.

Oh, for fuck sake.

'In this world there are three kinds of "what we know": what's revealed, what we discover, and what just is.'

'How do we know what "just is"? Don't we have to learn it by discovering it? By it being revealed to us?'

'Do you know how to breathe? How does your heart know how to beat?'

Sometimes we have to remind it: beat, damn it, beat.

'Okay. Point taken.'

'To determine your question, or questions, you need to figure out what is important to you.' He leans forward over his desk. We all try not to breathe in, but he has us, we're paying attention. 'So,' he pauses for dramatic effect, 'what do you want to discover?'

He sits down. Rubs his hands together. He's on to something here. He knows it. 'Take out your notebooks and tell me what your questions are. What questions will help you figure out what you want to know?'

I open to a new page. Look at Mr R, he looks back at me. He doesn't assume to know me or to be able to answer my questions or even assume to know my problems. He simply knows what it's like to be left.

This is easy. I've got nothing but questions.

Where is he? I mean really, where the hell is he? What in the world was he thinking? What is he thinking now? Has he once considered what this does to me? How can he do this to me? When is he coming back? How can I believe in anything? What's with his obsessions? The trains, the door, the keys? What else what else? What is strong enough to make him abandon his post? What am I with him here? What am I without him here? Why is this room so cold? How do I feel about Quiz? Is Jess a good friend or not? Or is she blowing me off because of a temporary boy? Will I grow up to be like Linden? Is that a good or a bad thing? Is my dad my real father? Does it matter? How do they get the trains to lean safely? Does the lake work in a cycle with the sun? Will it eventually take our house too? Why is Mrs Morse's roof black? Ditto with all the watertowers in the city? And do they make sense with the Chicago summers? What is my favorite food? Which lock is my dad's favorite? Where is he? Did he run off with Mrs R? What is it about the door and key that obsess him? It's just a door! How could he leave me? How can I stop him from leaving me again? How can I stop anyone from leaving me? Why don't chives die in the winter?

I take a breather, shake my hand out, look up. The class stares at me, everyone else long finished. Mr R giving me some time. I put my pen down. Mr R gives me a nod.

I sit in the back of the class. My shoulders shake. I've got questions. Lots of questions. I add two more. 'What if they don't leave any clues? What then?'

Palms to my eyes, chin to my chest. Did I say that out loud?

Mr R's glance is nothing, displaces nothing, but there's a heat to it. I'm hot from the inside, the blush building. The tears pushing forward, I will them down. Put my head down. Pull in my feet.

'Absence isn't perfection,' I say. 'It can't be.'

Everyone hears it. How can they not?

'Class dismissed,' he says.

'What about the bell?' Missy asks, staring at me.

'Since when have you obeyed the rules?' And so, even though the period has fifteen minutes to go, and he'll get his knuckles rapped, he shoos the rest of the class out of the room, and lets me sit, in the last row, feet, for once, curled beneath my seat, all by myself, unbothered, unharrassed.

When the bell rings Mr R leaves but I sit for longer. I sit through lunch when the room is empty and I'm tempted to sit through a junior calculus class that files in. But I don't. I drag myself down the hall to history.

I walk in, hand Mr Pavich the note. He looks down, then pushes out his arm and stops me from entering the room.

'I want an apology for the way you behaved in class on Tuesday. A note won't do it.'

I'm the one who deserves an apology.

'You've got to be kidding!'

'You've been disrespectful. That's unacceptable. In some countries they flog kids who talk back.'

Bet he'd like that. I bite my tongue. Keep it to myself. 'Give me the note.' I say. He looks at me blankly. I repeat it, put out my hand palm up.

'Give me an apology,' he repeats, his face beet-red. 'And you'll need to take the test after school today.'

'I have nothing to apologize for, I've done nothing wrong. Except the sin of not being that good at history, no wonder, with the help you give.' And to the class, 'Outta here. Bet he watches my ass as I go, the perv.'

The second step too far. And who cares? Life is too short. Countries fall, rulers are assassinated. The shit hits the fan, and the news hits the press.

The halls' walls have shiny tiles which alternate green and cream and a bit like throw-up. Hundreds of less shiny tiles make up the floors and they're high school filthy.

Mrs Melbourne doesn't even look up.

'It's you again.'

'He wants an apology.'

She looks at the clock. It's two-fifteen.

I hear him outside her office. 'A perv! She called me a perv!' The word rings and circles and reverberates. She doesn't look alarmed, but rather, faintly amused.

She goes out and closes the door behind her. They talk in whispers. I listen hard. 'She's being disciplined as we speak. You should be more understanding, her dad's disappeared.'

'What do I care!' he yells. 'She should be expelled. Expelled!'

'Alex.' Her voice is calm, I imagine she's placing a firm but gentle hand on his slimy arm. 'Go back to your class. She's switching classes anyway and you will not have to deal with her again.'

'I need an apology. Children cannot get away with such insolence.'

'Take deep breaths,' she says. 'Her record has been impeccable up to now. She's just going through a rough period.'

'Rough period, ha. This is the start of her decline. You're teaching her that she can get away with anything.'

Me and my dad. Getting away with it.

'Watch your language, Alex. I mean it. Forget this incident.'

She comes back in, refreshed. In balance, in control. Something in her is on my side.

'Roe, go to the library or take a break or something. Then go to your next class. I'll try to rush through the change. And… try to keep out of trouble.'

School is quiet between periods. I stop at Quiz's English class, put my hand up, he looks out. Winks. He's got practice today after school, maybe I'll see him tonight. After. Nothing to do, twenty minutes of the period left. I go and stand outside Mr Pavich's class and wait for the bell to ring. There's rustling and insolence. Whispers and he's ignoring it all. He's racing through some century, working himself up into a pop quiz. Jim Coran asks if he can slow down.

'Listen faster!' Pavich says, 'and shut-up!' and slams both hands down on the desk. A loud crack. The crash of a desk collapsing. The second one this term. The class falls completely silent. And stays that way until they burst from the room in loud punches of laughter.

When she sees me, Jess makes her lips into an OOOOO and shakes her hand in front of her. 'So how many days detention did you get?'

'Not a single breakfast club.'

'What?'

'Haven't you heard? My dad's missing. Poor me.'

'Poor you, my ass.'

'And what is your pretty ass up to after school?'

'I gotta go home. My dad's back from this week's trip. Mom and me are going to clean. Smile through dinner.'

'Call me later?'

'Sure thing. When the coast is clear.'

We knock knuckles together, clip our hips. And when she's halfway down the hall she yells, 'Don't be an orphan now, you hear!'

'Only if you won't be a slut!'

'Touché,' she yells back with a grin and a flourish of her hand.

Mrs Warner spots me from halfway down the hall. I race towards the door, but she corners me.

'Roe! Roe!'

She arrives with her tight round bun like a disused beehive on her head.

'Yes, Mrs Warner.'

'I heard that you misbehaved today.'

Misbehaved? What century is she living in?

'I had some difficulty with Mr Pavich.'

'I hear that you said some pretty bad things. Mean things to him.'

Whatever.

'I feel very strongly that you should apologize to him. He was just doing his job and you were being disrespectful and difficult.'

Is she for real? 'Mrs Melbourne says it's fine. I start a new class tomorrow.'

'Regardless. You should apologize. In writing.'

What, so he can hang that at the front of the room and have people pay homage to it? 'I don't need to do that.'

'I know that you're in a difficult situation at the moment. But that will pass and won't you feel bad that you took advantage of the situation and used it to be mean to people? What do you think your father would think?'

He'd think you're a stupid old bat. 'He'd think that Mr Pavich should apologize to me.'

'Roe Davis, I don't like the changes I'm seeing in you. You should really consider how you take on this challenge. Keep a positive mind and act positively in the world. You should use this situation to become a better person. Not a brat.'

Her eyes are falsely peaceful. Forced into a calm submission. She's half dead and she's one hundred per cent out of line.

I wish I knew the Bible or the Koran or something. Something about *until you've walked a mile in my shoes*. But I don't. Leaving seems like a good idea. And that's what I do.

The day almost feels like it's warming up. It's still well below zero but the wind's dropped, the lake will be still, the sky the color of summer water. The world inverted.

I take short-cuts home, hoping to avoid anyone I know and yet, still, through the curtains of the houses, pulled back like arched eyebrows, through the glances of women who unload children and groceries from big cars, from local workman who are fixing burst pipes and boilers, I feel their pity.

Everyone knows. How can they not know?

It's a suburb, behind closed doors and all that, and this development, about my dad, is meaty, and out in the open.

She's the one.

Abandoned.

He's gone, just up and left.

I heard there's no note.

I heard he's joined the merchant navy.

Wish I could do something like that. Leave it all.

How irresponsible.

And he left her to fend for herself.

She's adopted, you know. Twice abandoned.

From the start of our street I see Val the Vulture, who works at Village Hall, snooping around Mrs Morse's house. She mounts the stairs, stumbles, catches herself by grabbing onto the door handle. The bitch. She wouldn't, wouldn't. When she's steady, she rattles it, tries to get in. She moves to the window, scratches at the thick frost. If she could get it clear, she could see right through to the lake. But she won't be able to.

I'm standing in the middle of the street, equidistant between our houses, the path to the beach straight ahead. If I take a running leap, what would happen?

A loud burst of a siren makes me jump. A cop car. I step up and over the snow piled up the curb, crisp and now dirty. The cop parks in front of Mrs Morse's house and Val condemns the house with a single finger and gives me a small, evil wave. I cut up to my house, and she meets me before I even get to the stairs. Insect legs, but she moves like a flash.

It's 4:55 and the vulture has timed it perfectly. End of the business day. She's waving papers and the police officer next door is chomping at the bit to unfurl the tape.

'We won the appeal. Your dad had fourteen days to oppose this order. He's not done that.'

'He's not here,' I say.

'That's not our problem.' Behind her the cop stretches tape between trees, winds it tight, then to the porch. 'Keep out,' Val says, 'the crew and bobcats are coming on Friday.'

Tomorrow.

Last time they did this, my dad stormed the Village Hall. Waving papers, shouting elder abuse.

'It's too late,' Val says. 'If you lie down in front of the house, we won't bother to call the cops, we'll just roll over you. You'll be getting the demolition bill in the mail.'

The Vulture smiles and turns on her heels like a lieutenant. She doesn't look back. She drives away in a sleek grey Buick and the tape has gone up and I can't get my feet to move. And it's crystal clear to me I don't know how to play this game.

I toss my bag onto the porch and the tape is orange and sticky as I unwind its length. When it sticks in the fence, I tug and tug. It stretches thin but won't break, won't come undone. My butt is on the snow, cold through my tail bone. And I pull. Lean back, the fence angles a bit but the tape doesn't move. Mrs Taylor from across the street brings out scissors. She'll be thrilled, she'll have an open vista when this comes down. Until a replacement is thrown up. She's wrapped up warm. Busybody.

I will not be reduced to tears in front of her. I take the scissors. Smile, but not too friendly. It's tight.

'Watch yourself. They're sharp.'

Quick snips and I hand them back handles first.

'William will be home soon and I'm sure he'll help if you need any. It doesn't look like a one-person job.'

'Thanks. I'll do it myself.'

I crumple the tape further into a tight ball as I walk from tree to tree and then I walk across the property line and back into my house.

I take the stairs two at a time. Sixteen and I'm on the second floor landing, facing the open door to his bedroom. Linden's been sleeping in there but despite the racket of the other night, despite the fact that she's been in there for four nights, it looks nearly untouched. She's not made the bed (neither does my dad), but she's not moved a single thing from his dresser or from his nightside table except for the broken lamp which perches in two halves against the wall.

There's no time. I kneel down and pull a box from beneath the bed. I don't need to open it to know it's empty. I will not open it. I push it further into the room, out of the way.

I reach under and pull out a second, bigger box. This one is heavy and almost digs into the floorboards as I slide it out. I sit crosslegged and consider.

I've known that this box exists. Since forever. It's a simple shape, a box made to be a file for papers. The lock in front is simple, beautiful. Shaped like a door, the key is shaped like a door handle, made of ivory. There's a metal hook on the side where the key hangs. I won't need it.

My dad's house rules apply. Any lock can be opened. This box doesn't contain any secrets, only facts I don't know yet.

There are things you shouldn't know about your parents. Everyone knows that. Lauren was someone I did not need to know about in order to understand my dad. He'll probably tell me about her when I lose my first love. When I do something regrettable. When I flee one day without warning and come back just as suddenly.

There's too much here. Papers and papers and metal files and the usual. My dad's crap. Nothing that looks like a lawyer's number. I don't have time to scour every sheet. I can't wait. Night will be here soon. I need to salvage as much of the day as I can.

I call Linden. Get her answerphone. 'Phone the lawyer, any lawyer. The Village is tearing down her house. Linden. They're going to tear it down. Please please find help. Come home and help.'

I call Jess. Another message. And Quiz. He's still at practice. 'Come over. Now. Bring flashlights, gloves.'

Don't check in, don't hesitate. Don't pass go, do not collect two hundred dollars. Just arrive.

I can't wait for support. The key threatens to break in the lock of her front door and so once it's unlocked I leave it that way, fling open the door, move the couch to prop it wide, an old iron to hold the back door. A gale gusting through, driving, dry-powder of snow. I take arm loads full of her things and drop them in our living room. Fill up black bags, drawers.

I look around, trying to take time to choose wisely. I want my dad here. Now. To help. He'd know what to take. What had been important? What would help us to remember?

It's just twilight when headlights swing from Sheridan and onto Forsythia and a pickup crunches and slides around the corner. Carl opens the door and steps out in one smooth movement. He was a cowboy in a former life, like my dad. When he talks the air turns misty in front of him and then he walks through. Big, dark. Long strides.

'I just heard. That cow from the Village Hall came in bragging. I had to stop Carey from putting a gob into her celebratory mocha.' His arms are open wide, his eyes are on me and then on Old Mrs Morse's house. 'There's no way they'll succeed. We'll stop them.'

I put my hand on his forearm. My other in his hand. He looks down. Like a dad. Like an uncle. 'We can't, Carl.'

'Sure we can.' He pulls me into a hug. Strange stuff for strange times. Morphing borders. I step back. Pull my shoulders down, breathe. Remembering to breathe. Look at him. The coffee on his breath. Grounds under his fingers. The smell of onions and garlic from the cuff of his coat.

'Nope. They've got the right. Val says it's in violation of the building codes. My dad's been warned, and warned again. It's a public hazard.'

'That's BS. They're pushing their luck. When they come tomorrow we'll stop them. I'll put my truck in front of the porch.'

I put my arm back on his arm. 'It's going to come down, Carl. Without my dad, we just can't save it. It'd take a miracle. We've already had our reprieve. They've won their appeal.'

He snorts.

'Please help me salvage what we can.'

'Sure thing, Roe.'

Having Carl here helps me prioritize. I lead him to the living room. He moves past me into the room. 'Wow. Look at this thing.' He runs his hand over the craftsmanship of Morse's ancient door. 'I had no idea.'

'It was her father's. He built the old part of the house around it.'

'And she built a room around it.'

I nod. 'I suppose so.'

We work on the fittings, each with wrenches working at the bolts which keep it solid to the floor, then a hammer and a wedge we find down in the basement, hammered beneath its base which seems to have grown roots through the floorboards. Carl hammers, I hold the door and frame. Crack.

'That's a floorboard gone.'

I'm glad it's not the door.

We manoeuvre the door still in its frame out the back and carry it into my house. We prop it up against the wall opposite my dad's workspace.

'This your dad's stuff?'

'Yup.'

'Sort of…'

'Creepy, isn't it? Looks like it's just waiting for him to get to work.'

Carl gives me a short punch on my arm. 'No time to dawdle. I've got to close the café in an hour, and then pick up Sandy from the train.'

I follow him out of our house.

My arms ache. I've already got a cut on my leg from the corner of a table. My hands don't know whether to be tired or frozen. My neck pulls from the base of my skull down to my hips, tight like an overstretched rubber band. I know I'm salvaging all the wrong things. I know it and when Quiz arrives he won't go into the house at first.

'It doesn't seem right,' he says. 'What right do we have?'

Who needs this. Have some balls.

'This house is my dad's. She left it to him in her will. He'd want us to save as much as we can.'

Quiz still hesitates.

'Listen, Mrs Morse was like my grandmother. They'll be here with at least one bulldozer. With bobcats too. They may have to get out and bring parts down with axes. They're going to destroy her curved windows. Those beautiful windows. She's dead and no one has fought for her. They might even bring a wrecking ball.'

And with that he runs into the building like the most daring of firefighters. Quiz carries armloads of books, like they're children he's saving. By eight, when Carl leaves, an hour later than he should have, the three of us have carried out a lot of furniture: the door, the dining room table, a big bookshelf, the sideboard from the dining room, the coffee table, her bedside tables.

We put a few things inside our house, where we can find space, the rest of the furniture stands like people on the porch, jammed together so there's only a column of free space leading to the door. I wish our garage wasn't such a mess or we could put them there, a bit more protected.

'You'll have to move them inside soon. This cold will destroy them.'

'We'll do it ASAP.'

We haven't saved the beds, or the dresser from upstairs, although we manage to save filled drawers, perfume bottles, 1950s Old Spice bottles (empty), housecoats, robes, her silver, her pressure cooker, her baking sheets.

We wave to Carl as he backs out of the drive and Quiz pulls me into a

Elizabeth Reeder

hug. Kisses my hair. 'Shouldn't you take a break? Stop even. You won't be able to save it all.'

I step away. His hanging arms. His small resolve. My hard face.

'You look tired,' he adds.

'Go home, Quiz. Just go.'

'I didn't mean...'

'I know what you meant. I'm fine.'

Softer words, but I don't walk the two steps towards him, I don't pull him close. My battle. My sore arms.

He carries a few more boxes but when his mom phones to see where he is, he shrugs his shoulders and goes. In times like these you know who your friends are. It's easy to be there when it's smooth. Him falling asleep and us folded into each other and my arm draped over him so he's safe and protected. What we all want. Safety. A haven. Home. He doesn't want a girlfriend with big problems: a lost dad, a destroyed house. Responsibilities. Shit, I don't want them either.

Jess never shows up. Doesn't leave a message. I never ask her for anything. Never. And she's not bothered her ass to help me the one time I do.

Linden arrives at 8:30.

'Sorry I'm late Roe.'

She should have been here hours ago. If she had her priorities right. I see the dark circles under her eyes. Big deal. Who cares.

As she fits her headlamp, she rambles on, 'What a totally wasted day. The pipes burst at the gallery, luckily none of my work got it, but a whole corner needs fixed and rebuilt and painted. And the framers messed up. They ripped one of my photographs, a big one. I'm screwed.'

I walk past her with a box of odds and ends. We don't have many boxes so I load them up and then take stuff out in the living room. Re-use the box. When I come back out she starts in again.

'I left a few messages with a lawyer I know. He should get back to us. I tried a few others, no one was about.'

She should have got home addresses. Pounded on doors. Her exhibition is eight days away. This is now. This is a house, this is someone we love, this matters more than some stupid pictures. And there's no way we've done enough to save it.

Eventually she realizes I don't give a shit about talking. Then we carry and carry and carry. Headlamps around our thick skulls leave our hands free. The world closes in. Limited view. Move move move. Clear out the house. Clear out.

It's nearly eleven when my phone vibrates. It takes forever to fish it out from beneath all the layers of clothes. It's Jess.

'Roe, could you come round and sort of, you know, distract my dad…'

Mr Carmichael's voice so loud it sounds like he's taken the phone, 'Get off that phone, Miss. Now!' His voice fades a bit, as if he's turned his attention to something else. 'And you…'

'I can't, Jess, I've got my own stuff to do. You can come here if you need to.'

The line goes quiet.

'Please, Roe.'

It's a plea I've not heard before.

There's far more still in this house than our house. All this beautiful furniture, all her pictures and books.

'I can't. I've got my own shit to deal with.'

'Okay,' she says.

'He's a bastard,' I say. All that ranting and raving. All the walking on glass Jess and her mom do. What can I do about it? She knew that the tattoo would piss him off.

'It's the stress of his job, all the travel.' Jess has said this before. And having a daughter that pushes all his buttons.

'How does the tatoo look?'

'Absolutely fantastic,' she says, laughing.

The phone goes dead.

'Who was that?'

'Jess. Her dad's going a bit crazy. She got a tattoo.'

'She's only fifteen.'

'Nearly sixteen.'

Linden smiles. 'A tattoo is a big deal.'

'It's just an excuse, Linden.'

I go up to Mrs Morse's bedroom. It's when I start to take out the drawers of her dresser that I see another picture. It's slid out of its frame and into the rickety drawer. Face down. There's my dad, a woman, and a baby. Me. No time for this. I pocket it to look at it later.

Under the bed there's one box I find. It doesn't hold secrets, I know this. It's a pair to my dad's box, this one without the knot but concaved in towards the boxy shape, marking the knot's absence. The box sounds empty. But the very existence of it holds facts. A history. Her history. I carry it next door and slide it under my bed. I get the one from my dad's bedroom and put it there too. Side by side, it's unmistakeable: they've been made from the same wood at the same time.

Did my dad plan, while he was making them, to give one to Mrs Morse? For a purpose? Or was it simply a gift he gave later on because she'd admired it?

I go back over to her house. Linden is sorting linens. I'm hoping she has memories too. Can help us save the right things. What are the right things?

But Mrs Morse was never Linden's lover's mom.

When we're packing her linens up into bags Linden reminisces. 'A nice old lady. Sort of, well, old. With her overgrown garden, her good cookies. That's about it. It's hard to think about this house gone.'

Even I have more insight than that.

I don't know if they'll bulldoze the shed too, so I just try to get as much of the garden stuff out of there as I can and chuck it to the other side where I imagine the property line to be. I plan to stand there all day as they wreck it.

There's snow blown all over the floors. Frost on every surface. I can't feel my toes, or my fingers. My nose is so red, it's white. I'd cry, but the tears would just freeze there, at the corners of my sore eyes.

We're far from done but can't really do anymore.

It's after one when we stop. Linden makes tacos with the help of spices out of a packet. She hands me a beer. Protein, and more protein, and a cold that heats me up.

We don't really talk. Eat just enough to get us through the night. The night that is a perfect black outside. We climb over piles of Mrs Morse's stuff to get to the couch and once there I put my feet up on her lap and she rubs them back into life.

'I lied to Duncan on Monday,' I say.

'I do that all the time.'

'I'm serious.' She bends my foot back at the ankle, makes small circles on the ball of my foot. 'I moved a box; it was important to dad. There's no secrets in it. I'm pretty sure it's empty. It's just dad's. I feel like if I open it, I banish him.' There'll be no reason for him to come back. The house, me, nothing will be his anymore.

'Roe, nothing you do will change when he comes back. He'll come back soon, when he's ready.'

I shrug my shoulders. Kiss her cheek, give her a small hug.

I set my alarm and lie on my bed with my eyes open. Today the universe has just taken, taken, taken.

Dad's there. Just at the edge of my vision. I'm upstairs asleep and he's back at the table. He has a sheet of paper and a pen. His hand hovers. He tries but not too hard to put it into words. His tears are hot and slow. Thick. He crumples the paper and once he's gone, he leaves nothing behind.

The wind whips through the house. Branches break off, hit the roof. Ice creaks down by the lake and I'm aware of the sensation, like life itself. It's something like strength, like having and wanting at the same time.

I want this. Her house to be alive again. Full of the force of the weather. For Mrs Morse to be here feeding me cookies. The bottom of her braid curling in. Her body slow, deliberate and distinctly birdlike. Sometimes she moves with the aches of age, sometimes she's light as a girl.

I want this. The lake further out. I want it to be summer and full of heat. And I want my dad arguing with me about whether I can have a beer or whether he'll take me out driving.

'I've got my license,' I say.

'Provisional,' he says.

'It's what it's made for. I drive just fine.'

'Sure you do,' he says, patting my arm, 'for a maniac.'

'I'm your maniac and you need to take me out to practice.'

But he can't bring himself to do it more than occasionally. His hand holding the handle above the passenger's seat door, bracing himself on the dash. And only on holidays when local roads are dead. I'm months behind. Sixteen in three weeks and hardly any hours on the road. And my dad, scared of exactly what I might do to his shiny baby of a car.

I want him here, without a hint that he's ever been gone, without a hint he'll ever leave again.

Fear, it was fear in Jess's voice. I bolt up in bed. All the sounds different. The world getting ready for some extra space. A hollow. Voices from the beach, clearer, nearer. Why didn't I realize? I phone Jess. Hoping she has her phone on vibrate.

After two rings she picks up.

'Jess, it's me.'

'Hey babes.' She's calm and cool.

'You okay?'

'Emergency over,' she says.

'Do you want me to come over? Or do you want to come here?'

'Nah, it's okay,' she says. She pops her gum. I'm not sure Jess ever really sleeps.

'Are you sure?'

'Yup.'

'See you tonight?'

'I don't know, Roe. I'll have to see.'

'Try to get some sleep.'

'You too my deer.'

'Ha ha ha.'

FRIDAY

With the doors swung wide open, the house welcomes in the new day. The sun low, only ever low this time of year. Weak too, but clean and icy.

The machines arrive and I rush out camera in hand. Linden is beside me holding a digital video camera she 'borrowed' from the school. We bring the workmen coffee and doughnuts. It's not their fault they have a shit job. That they're destroying an old woman's house. They move around talking and pointing; they're sheepish when they look at us and I catch them looking behind us towards the busy street. For salvation? Towards an escape?

At the last minute just before the scoop takes the heart out of the building I run forward, yelling.

'Wait, stop, wait. WAIT!'

And they do. Expectant. Hopeful I hold a reprieve. No such luck. I turn back to Linden.

'The front door!'

Mrs Morse's front door is beautiful. I should have thought about it yesterday. Mahogany, deeply stained, repeatedly protected. A thin strip of stained glass on the top. Four separate frames: the lake in each season.

One of the wrecking crew is out of the cab, screwdriver in hand.

'I'm Ward,' he says to me, shakes my hand. 'Bill, get over here and help me with this.'

Although they leave the engines running, they have it off the hinges in a matter of minutes. Ward is flushed, I swear he has tears in his eyes.

'I've always loved this house.'

'Me too,' I say as I take the door from his hands and Linden takes it from Bill's. We carry it towards our house and lean it against the garage. I'm nice. Too nice.

When they crush the curved windows I swear it's my breastbone that's cracked. When the slates of the roof shatter and splinter, I can't get my hands to steady. I'm so cold, my toes must be blue in my boots. I know this. The ground is cut, upset. Her garden ripped through with tire tracks, great big gashes of meanness.

I go inside our house. I sit and watch from the safety of the kitchen.

What will my dad say?

How many times can I let him down? In how many ways?

I should have chained myself to the front porch. Gone to jail for something I believe in. If not for this house, then what will I ever fight for? Would I have been enough to stall them? To stop them?

And I didn't even try.

Some random lawyer arrives too late, half the house already gouged out. Empty-handed to boot.

Val the Vulture hasn't showed up. Although she's probably filming it secretly so she can watch it in the privacy of her own home. Like porn. It takes a sickeningly short amount of time. From the moment of sun-up, until not quite three o'clock. Which is when she comes to gloat. Val stalks the property, and it takes her all of ten seconds to see the shed. The guys and their big machines have left the garden shed untouched. But she's too late and the machines have already left, holding up traffic on Sheridan on their way to wherever they call home, brick dust and wood splinters of Mrs Morse's home caught in the cracks and edges of their bodies.

'Too close to the property line to call,' Ward had said.

I swear that if she'd had an axe she'd have taken it to the walls herself. I know that one day soon a little bobcat, with a driver with an apologetic face and nod, will scoop it up and leave a pile of planks.

When Val leaves I go to the shed and take off that door too, which is more space than wood, with only a knotted twine pull for a door handle.

And the shack gets to stay. At least for a night.

Dear Mrs Morse,

They bulldozed your house today. We saved some of your papers. And your doors (of course). I've got your housecoat. Your cooking mitts. I did a crap job. I just didn't know what to save. I miss you. There's a gap where your house used to be. I miss it too. And dad. He's been gone for a week now. I miss him. I wonder who will see him first, you or me.

I put the paper in a bottle and put it on the windowsill in the kitchen and wait for a thaw or a trip to the sea.

I pull the photo from my coat pocket. Something gained, please. Something given and found, today. Please.

It's my mom with me as a baby. A toddler. Arms open. Both of us facing each other. My mother, knees bent, body forward, arms open, mine in imitation of hers. Hers starting to come together in a clap. Faces bright as light. Center of the universe, a sun. The green grass, my mother's bare arms, the curve of her breasts in her bright pink tank top, her tanned muscular arms. The total love in her face. Focused on me.

Linden and I make salami sandwiches and they taste horrible. We leave the crusts and other bits.

'Roe, I'm going to have to go to work. This show is only a week away and it's a mess. I'm going to call Mel and Duncan and have them spend the night with you. I don't think you should be alone.'

'Please don't call them. I'll be fine.'

'You can't stay here alone.'

'Why not?'

'I just don't think it's a good idea. It's been a tough week.'

'Well you should stay then. I don't want him in the house.'

'He means well.'

'Does he? Isn't this just his chance to be superior. To prove that his boring, conservative choices are righter, better than my dad's irresponsible choices? Won't he just come here to gloat?'

'Roe. He's quite upset.'

'And jealous. And a bit victorious. He and dad have barely spoken for years. Mel's the go-between. I'm fifteen, not stupid.'

'I've never said...'

'Then don't treat me like I am. I'll be fine alone tonight. Don't worry if you can't make it back. If you find a piece of ass. Don't worry. Go for it. It's just my dad who's gone. No worries. He's done it before. It will all be FINE.'

I slam out the door. Walk. Pound my feet. I'm full up. Furious. She doesn't know what she's doing. It's a mess. This stupid, stupid, ugly wasteground. It's all a mess.

I go round and round the neighborhood. Go to school. Walk around the track. It's deserted. It's after eight. I try to phone Jess but there's no answer. And then I try Quiz.

'Hiya.'

'Hi, Roe.'

'What are you up to?'

'Nothing much.'

'Thanks for phoning today. It was good to know you cared.'

'I thought you'd be at school. And then I forgot.'

Give them what they want and you're so quickly forgotten. Don't rise to it. Don't get riled. He's a sixteen-year-old boy. Easily distracted.

'I'm going to be alone at home for a while, do you feel like hanging out? We could...'

'I'm just going to a rugby party. We're voting for captain. It's important that I go,' he says.

'That sounds fun. Want to come and pick me up?'

'No girls allowed.'

There's no way that his voice is nearly apologetic enough. No this. No that. No answer. No friends. A boyfriend who's not worth much either.

'Well I'm going to a party where no assholes are allowed.'

'Roe?'

My phone beeps. I have another call.

'Bye Quiz.'

'Hi, Roe.'

'Hiya.' I'm relieved. Jess. 'Any parties tonight?'

'Roe and a party. The world's gone topsy turvy.'

'Absolutely. So where are you going tonight?'

'Get off that phone! I've warned you!' Jess's dad, loud. She whispers, 'I'll be at yours as soon as I can.' And she hangs up.

I head home and when I get there, Linden's car is gone. And there's a gaping hole where a house used to be.

Last winter, Jess and me on Morse's roof. An ice storm has left everything sparkling. Mrs Morse still alive, in her house making dinner. It's cold, but just November or something. I'd never have climbed onto a roof of my own free will.

'But it's better done in company,' Jess says.

'Can't we wait 'til spring?'

'No can do missy. Now or never.'

'Can't I choose?'

'Now!' she shouts and whispers at the same time. Morse will kill us if she catches us.

It's like there's a map on the outside of the house: foothold, handhold, foot hand. Jess sees it. And I don't.

'Did you used to be a monkey?' I ask her.

'Watch and mimic.'

She moves and I try to judge where to put my foot, what will help me move up, but I move to the side, up the building and down again, trying to get sense of it.

She sits with her legs hanging over the side of the gutters, in the short flat before it gets steep.

'Jess it's just too hard. I can't see the way up.'

'Wimp. Get your butt up here.'

She chips at the icicles that hang off the roof and starts tossing them over the edge at me. One bounces off my hat, one off my sleeve. Her aim gets better and better and one, like an arrow, goes down the inside of my jacket, sweater too and I have ice melting down my back.

'Oi, like that'll help.'

'They can only make you faster.'

Foot, hand, foot hand. My chin even with her knees. Triumph.

'Get down here right now!' Morse yells. 'You two should know better. You get yourselves killed on my property and I'm liable. Roe,' she says, 'you should know better.' Her voice full of disappointment, but a small smile graces her lips.

I pull myself up onto the roof. Look down at her between my legs. She shakes her head and goes inside. Jess walks along the edge of the roof. Surveying the world. 'I can see my house,' she says.

Elizabeth Reeder

I sit with a cold, wet butt. Proud of myself.

Jess shimmies down to the ground in about a second. It takes me ages to get over the edge of the roof, my legs shaking, that nerve-wracking moment of turning around.

Later I bring Morse a small ceramic tile I made in art. It has a sprig of lavender embedded in the glaze. 'I'm sorry,' I say.

She smiles. 'I didn't think you had it in you. Want to clean the gutters next year?'

I pour myself a whisky and Coke. I shudder with each sip. I hate the stuff. Read Linden's lame note. Blah blah blah. Work. Time to think. Back tomorrow morning. Blah.

The door opens. A huge gust of wind. Jess arrives without a coat, looking windswept and flabbergasted.

'Holy shit. Roe. Holy shit. No way.'

She's at the window, shaking her head. 'I didn't expect, I hadn't imagined, it'd be so, so…'

'Completely gone.'

She nods. 'The whole thing.'

'Except the shed.'

'How generous of them.'

'It'll come down too.'

'You have anything to drink?'

'Absolutely.' I hand her mine. She downs it. I fill my dad's hipflask. She nods approval.

'And now about that outfit you've got on.' She takes a long swig and then puts me into a silly short and tight dress.

'I'll freeze.'

'But you look great.'

She makes me wet my hair again and she styles it, so the curls are full and black.

We drink the scotch straight. It burns and my head is clearer, but flying a bit. And that's what I'm after.

'You have a jacket I could borrow?'

'Sure thing.' I give her my long black coat. I wear my oilskin coat.

'Rounds out that outfit nicely. Do you want some leg warmers to go with that?'

'Ha ha. Who cares? I'll be cold enough as it is. No one will remember what I arrive in.'

'That's all they'll remember.'

Although Jess and I arrive late she's caught up with the party and Kevin's tonsils in no time. And then there's fireworks between Kevin and his girlfriend, and Jess stands with me, our arms hooked, our shoulders pressed together, heads in, laughing and gossiping and watching the fight intently.

They make hand gestures in Jess's direction, their body language is stiff and distant. Furious. By the end of the night Jess is kissing Tim and Kevin's alone without a girlfriend and without Jess.

I'm used to sitting alone. Prefer it. Especially if it means I can be invisible. Jason sits down beside me. I don't try to shirk him. Maybe I've misjudged him, because he doesn't say much. Just sits there, gets me a new drink once in awhile.

While Jess is kissing Tim, Jason says to me, 'She's a free spirit that one, isn't she?'

'Do you wish it was you?'

'No, I don't want to be a girl.'

'Why, you'd have such lovely legs.'

He stretches his thick footballer's leg out. Pouts.

'I meant, kissing her.'

'No,' he says. 'I wouldn't want that.' And leaves it there. No big gesture. Nothing.

When our glasses are empty, I toss them behind us. There's a wasteland already over the living room. Someone has a major clean-up job tomorrow before the parentals come home. Our legs have been touching for ages. Quiet like. Unassuming. He's not made any move. He's either v. confident or v. patient or v. arrogant or v. uninterested.

I don't care. I lean in and he tilts his head and there's something small and insecure between us. Harder. Meaner. He tugs at the waist of my dress to pull me closer and even though it's ugly, stiffer, and even though he tastes like baby aspirin and French fries, we sit there necking.

When he goes to the bathroom, I slide down off my perch. Jason high-fives his friends on the way to the john. I glance at Jess who's having the time of her life. She's free. Wreckage strewn behind her. And it's not her problem.

I go out the back door. I run all the way home. In stupid shoes, and a silly dress hiked up nearly to my hips. Jumping over hedges, skirting rose bushes, and running until the cold is like daggers in my lungs, until I can't breathe. Until I am barely conscious of being me at all.

It's a clean break. One day I'm supposed to be this thing and the next day I am simply no longer this thing. I am another thing. I need to go back. I want to be back there, where I am no longer this thing. No longer abandoned.

He's quit. Me. His jobs. As locksmith and as dad. What is left if you quit one thing and go in search of another? Is the first thing simply knocked out of the picture because there's no room anymore? He says I'm his pumpkin pie. The apple of his eye, the center of his universe.

And I don't care about any of it. Not for a single reason he can come up with. He could be dead somewhere, murdered. Hit by a car, mugged in the city. He could have lost his memory. Or his mind. And I don't care. He could have the best reasons in the world.

'I did it for you, Roe,' he'll say, 'they said they'd kill you if I didn't go away. It was me or you,' he says. 'I saved you.'

And I'll slap him. I imagine it. A slap like a crack. A handprint on his cheek. And he'll know.

I re-read Linden's note.

Thought you could use some space. I'll be back tonight or tomorrow morning. To help open the shop. I'm sorry about tonight. Love, Linden.

Her love looks like a bird.

The boys who come to visit the demolition site at night have sharp edges, these fronts they wear. They creep around the wasteland that's Mrs Morse's plot of land. Take a piss like dogs. I imagine their privates shrinking in the cold but it's some sort of hormonally charged contest and they won't be defeated. I expect laughter but it doesn't come. There's a reverence in how they mark the territory. I imagine the trinkets left behind: piss and zipper pulls and spit. Homage to a witch.

SATURDAY

It's five a.m. and I'm running. Jess's voice had been controlled, in that way where if you let even the smallest amount of emotion through, you'll be a wreck. The ground is hard and icy but I run anyway. The world dark and silent and still. The roads might be safer but this path is always, in any season, faster. I just want her to hold on until I get there. I don't know what I'm going to find.

The garage door is wide open, as is the door to the house. Both cars gone. The spare key I carry won't be needed. Music blares from upstairs.

He's gone.

Upstairs, there's blood in the hall. Classic crime scene. Footprints, splatter, handprints. The frenzy of music is so loud I almost can't focus. Her door is closed, I try the handle, push on it. It's locked. I yell. 'It's me, Jess. It's Roe.'

It takes forever, but I hear the lock click and I slowly push the door open. Jess is leaning against the wall and as I step into the room she slides down to sitting. Her face is a mess, a gash across her cheek, blood from the edge of her mouth and she's got the heel of her hand jammed up against there to staunch the flow. Her shirt is ripped and I see marks on her shoulders and on the knuckles of her hand, one of her nails is torn right down low and it's bleeding too.

She's trying to hold washcloths over the wounds on her cheek but they're sodden and they keep slipping. Blood is coming from somewhere,

Elizabeth Reeder

everywhere?

'Oh Jess, what's happened?'

Her face is pale. I stand there talking to her like nothing's wrong. Pretend it's fine and it will be. She's barely able to stay sitting, even with the wall for support. I don't recognize whatever it is that's blaring. Despite the noise, the house is hollow. I turn off the music. Then it's truly, eerily quiet.

'Roe, help.'

I have no clue what to do. I look at her, bring her another washcloth, hold it to her head.

'Phone an ambulance.'

Shit. Of course. I pat my pocket, I've forgotten my phone. 'Where's the phone?'

'I don't know. I dropped it.'

I look around. 'You do have the messiest room in the world.'

'Not now, Roe.'

'I'm going to the kitchen phone. Will you be okay?'

I don't wait. I run down the stairs, dial 911.

'We need an ambulance. 533 Cherry Oak Street.'

'What's happened?'

'I don't know. She's all cut up, having trouble breathing, can't get her standing.'

I turn and hang up the phone. There's a crushed lamp and shattered plates. There's no blood but it's like the violence has snuck out the door and wreckage has been left behind.

Jess has slid down a bit closer to the floor. Her eyes are closed. The bleeding really doesn't seemed to have slowed.

Jess. Jess. I hold the towel which has slipped. Her left wrist is gashed. Wrist to halfway to her elbow.

Jess and me, eight years old, her watching as I ride no-handed and nearly wreck my knee for good; the next year we're climbing the tree out back when I break my nose and get a black eye. At ten, I break my leg water-skiing when her folks take us away to Trout Lake up in Wisconsin. It's like I do everything accident prone and violent so she doesn't have to. But now, with this, she's trumped me. I wish I could do this for her.

The blood. Gashes right up her arm. I touch her face. She starts to cry.

'You have no idea,' she says.

Now I do, maybe. A bit. And she didn't tell me what was going on.

Never hinted.

I'm calm, like someone's taken my heart and I'm dead and yet walking, and they let me ride in the ambulance. I've pulled the phone numbers off the fridge, thinking, how do I get in touch with her mom? How do I get the police to go after her violent mean as a dog dad?

Her eyes are full and empty and it's only later when I see the vivid color of the welts on her back, the backs of her legs, the burn bruises on her wrists that I really understand. I shouldn't see these things, but I do.

'You can come and live with me,' I say to her as we ride in the ambulance, 'just you and me.'

At the hospital I give the list of phone numbers to some administrative nurse. 'Don't call her dad or let him know where she is. Try to find her mom.'

It's the first time ever that I'm in a better state than her. Despite everything. I don't know what to say to her.

'Hey fellow orphan, take a load off.' Her face is bruising as she speaks and she grimaces more than smiles but she sounds just like herself. Looks just like her. She's got some broken ribs, a bruised lung, and her left wrist is shattered. She has seven stitches across her cheek, and another seventeen on her arm. 'Lucky seven,' she says, and touches her cheek. 'I've no idea what seventeen means.'

She sits in bed while a cop asks her questions. She wants me there, fights to have me there. I hold her hand and don't flinch.

'He's never done anything like this before,' she says. 'He comes home on Thursday and it's like someone else is in my dad's body. He rants, throws a lamp, slams stuff. Rants more. Mom placates him and they make up.'

That's why she didn't come to help with Morse's stuff.

'In the morning we all go about the normal routines. I go to school. They go to work. At night, they start to fight, I say they fight, but really dad goes ballistic and mom grabs her keys, saying she'll get help as she runs for the door. My dad glares at me and I lock myself in my room. I don't doubt that my mom will be back soon and so after a bit I slide down the roof like usual and go to Roe's. I figure mom will have brought the police, sorted it, by the time I get home.'

'What time was that?'

'Four a.m., or something. Maybe five. I think she'll have sorted it, but she hasn't. I don't know why. Don't know. He's waiting, boozing and god knows what else because my real dad isn't there. There's a fucking monster in his place. Crazy. Calling me by my mom's name. Calling me a whore. "You're my wife or you're dead," he keeps saying. I keep telling him that it's me, Jess. His daughter.'

"You're a whore too," he says.

'I fight back. The bastard. Somehow I manage to get him out of my room and lock the door. I tell him I'm phoning the police. I tell him he's the whore. He's the stinking two-faced liar of a whore.'

I'm grateful that her house doesn't have a no locked lock policy like mine.

'Who the hell does he think he is? He'll have a black eye, and a limp. When you find him. Why aren't you out there arresting his ass?'

The police officer, a good looking twenty-something, who is well out of his league, says, 'Stick to the facts miss, if you can.'

'You can stick the facts up your ass,' Jess says. 'Your pretty ass,' she adds. Inappropriate. All Jess. He leaves, flustered. And we laugh. And then we sort of lean together, holding each other up.

Her mom arrives and when she comes in to see Jess, I have to go sit outside with the lawyer she's brought. Turns out the car broke down before she could get to her sister's. She didn't have a cent. Blah blah blah. She left her daughter at home with a madman. What in the world was she thinking?

There's blood everywhere. It's under my nails, in blotches over my shirt, on the arm of my coat. I'm sure there's stuff in my hair too. Mrs Carmichael is pristine. She had time to shower anyway. If you look like a mess, your life is a mess. She looks neat and clean. Her life is perfect.

She gives me a ride home in her sister's Mercedes. The smell of cigarettes in the upholstery. She smells like Shalimar.

It's not her fault. Not her fault. She's losing her family, her husband's a raging maniac. She fled for her life and should have saved her daughter too and here she is looking perfect. Her mascara is not running.

There's the possibility that they both could have died. 'You're mine or you're dead,' he'd said.

'Thank you for what you did today, Roe.'

'Jess needed me. I was there.'

Too late. I was there too late. She didn't trust me enough to tell me she needed me earlier. But I was there, eventually.

'I don't know what would have happened without you.'

She'd have died. That's what. Because you weren't there. I look at her. She's not at ease. She's worried. Her thick makeup might be hiding bruises too. I don't care.

'She'd be dead,' I say.

'Maybe,' she says. 'He usually pulls it together. He was angry at me, he usually doesn't pull Jess into it.'

Usually? This has happened before? Has she seen the house? The blood, the footprints in blood, the handprints on her daughter's wrist and neck?

'Shouldn't you have stayed around to find out?'

'Shouldn't you have respect for your elders?' We turn onto Forsythia. 'Oh my god.' She brakes hard, skids a bit. Mrs Morse's house is a chunk of dirt with a shed in the corner of the plot. Her hands are at ten and two on the wheel. Her knuckles defined by bones.

'Shouldn't you take your parental duties seriously?' I open the door and remove my messy body from the car. I leave behind bits of her daughter's blood on the seat and the door handle. I put my head back in the car, my eyes full of tears. 'Please try to keep her safe. She's important to me.'

The door closes softly. Like solidness itself. She'll land on her feet. Will Jess be beside her?

I take my clothes off as soon as I'm in the door. A pile on the floor. I take the steps upstairs two at the time. A hot hot shower. Wash my hair. Follow the directions. Rinse. Repeat. Five minute miracle conditioner but I can't wait that long. And I'm out in a minute, smelling of roses. Pink skinned. Safe. Lucky.

I twist my hair up, still wet. Dripping. No time. I should have been at the shop hours ago. It should already be closed again after serving customers with a smile. I dress in sweatpants and running shoes. Two sweatshirts, and a fleece. A big thick hat. Gloves.

I want to find my dad. To bring him home. So I can punch him. Yell at him at the top of my lungs.

I want to kick walls. To scream. To fuck until I'm sore. To find a punch bag and make it weep stuffing.

I want Jess to sit with me in the car and tell me what happened. In her own words. Just between her and me. No cop present. But they keep her in for a few days, for evaluation, for her own safety, until they can assess whether or not 'home' is safe for her.

I've had enough. I've risen to the occasion. Okay dad. This little excursion of yours has been fun and all, but enough. You've got responsibility. You have a daughter who needs you. How dare you. A day was enough. A week is too much.

Our house trembles. I'm sure this is what Old Mrs Morse felt. Our house isn't under threat or anything. When the lake rages again, whenever that might be, quite a few bigger, more expensive houses across the road will come in for it first, and the Village is sure to act on their behalf.

At some point there was a fence between us and Mrs Morse but the car tore it down and so now we can, literally, stand on the edge of a precipice.

I'm standing at the edge yelling at the top of my lungs.

Come home. Come home.

Look at all we've lost. We've lost Mrs Morse and her house. We've lost. I've lost.

I stretch my hamstrings against Mrs Morse's aspen. At least they left her trees. Then I stretch my Achilles' tendons. Circle my hands and arms above my head. I run into town. On my way, I pass a small bobcat and a flat bed 4x4 which have come to knock down the shed. When I come home Mrs Morse's plot will be a nothing but a flat square of frozen dirt and snow so dirty it looks like dirt.

It's a quick sprint, ten minutes tops. Smooth ice on the sidewalks but the grass is more solid, crunches underfoot. When I can, I run in the street. Small splatters of dry ice and melted ice up the backs of my calves.

I can barely get the door of my dad's shop open. There's a pile of mail and handwritten notes. I drop the pile on the counter and blast the heat. It takes about two minutes to warm the place up. As I start to thaw out, my hair drips and I use one my dad's hand towels from the back of the shop to wipe off my neck.

There are ten messages on the answerphone and I know I should listen to them. I know this.

I turn the sign from closed to open, and remove the totally misleading handwritten sign about this morning's opening. I'm about to start to read the notes when the door chimes.

It's Carl. 'Didn't think you were going to make it today.'

I open the Styrofoam box he's packed; he's brought me a cheeseburger and fries. He hands me a cup.

'Cherry Coke,' he says. It'll be the stuff he makes, real Coke, his own cherry syrup. The burger and fries are steaming. He's put in two little thimble cups of ketchup. Who'd have thought that Carl would be the only one here for me? My eyes start to fill. I will not cry. Will not cry.

'I almost didn't make it.'

'It was busy earlier.'

Like a friend, he ignores the welling and I blink, gain control.

'Sort of glad I missed it. I don't know what I'd say. It was a stupid idea to open the shop.'

'Some people really need their keys. They've asked if you could give them to me and they'll drop by later.'

I laugh. My own little storm in my own little teacup. 'I was thinking people would come by to leer.'

'There were a few of those, too.'

I attack the burgers and fries.

'Whoa there, Roe. Take time to chew.'

'I didn't have breakfast.'

'That's not like you. What's up?'

My best friend nearly died. Her dad is still on the loose. My aunt forgot she's supposed to look after me.

'I had to deal with something.'

'That sounds mysterious.'

I let the topic disappear as I eat and drink. Carl is one of those strong silent types, minimal conversationalist when faced with high-strung emotion.

'Carl, do you ever want to go and search for your lion?'

'Maybe a bit, on bad days. But really, it's just something I enjoy reading about, researching. Survival, beauty. That sort of stuff. Some people have tennis or golf or stamps, I've got this.'

'But why don't you go in search of it?'

'Because it's a hobby, Roe. It's not something I have to do, not now anyway. It's something I could do if I didn't love the diner so much; if I didn't love Sandy and Tony.'

He stays because he loves his family. Loves his job. I wipe my hands on my sweatpants.

'There's a napkin here.' He holds up a red and white checked thing.

I want to get out of here. 'Okay, who wants their keys?'

He pulls out a piece of paper and reads off the names while I find the keys and the paperwork. They're all there. Thankfully my dad's good at his job.

I lock the door behind us.

I stand on tiptoes and kiss Carl on the cheek, his hands full of other people's keys. 'Thanks, Carl.'

He crosses the street, turns and yells, 'Don't be a stranger!'

I run in and out of streets, taking a long, roundabout way home. There are families everywhere, getting in and out of cars. Laughing, laden with sleds and cross-country skis. Wrapped up warm. Big thermoses of hot chocolate. Handmade scarves around kids' necks. Hanging down their backs. Big happy families everywhere.

My nose burns with every breath I take in, my lungs are sharp and tight. I'm unfit. The wind blasts shards through my sweatpants. I run hard, faster than I should. My street is quiet. I'm alone. I run full pelt past the black dirt and leafless trees on her lot. It looks abandoned. Let down. All the liquid in my body has frozen. The house is hot when I crash inside, still running. I trip over the pile of my clothes. Nearly hit my head on the kitchen table. Catch myself and my hand slaps the counter instead. My ankle is slightly twisted. I regain my balance and I hit the counter again and again. Make a fist. I hit it so hard I think I might have broken the bone. I pull myself up. Pull off some layers. I walk around like a caged animal. This place is a garbage pit. A mess. And none of it is my mess. I haven't created any of this. How was I supposed to prevent this? Be pink perfect? The good girl? I am that. Big lot of good that does. All these things I don't know. Can't know, can't fix. Locks. Build this. Save this. Destroy this. He thinks he can leave and it will all be the same when he comes back, when he deigns to take some responsibility. Well, he couldn't be more wrong.

On the wall is a corkboard. Filled with all the things we need to tell each other, we need to remember. Some fat lot of good that did, where the hell was the lawyer's number when we needed it? Where is the note he should have left about where he's gone? I yank it down, the nail pulling out of the wall. I chuck the nail towards the trash, miss and it bounces off the wall. I put the board on the table, on top of all the shit already there. I pull off every last scrap of paper, every carryout menu, every phone number, with and without names. The board is empty. Pocked. My dad made this board out of wine corks. Fucking wonderful. I crack it over my knee. A crevice down the middle and then the corks scatter, mixing with all the thumbtacks: flat and silver, and high plastic ones, shaped like bells, clutter the floor. Finally. A mess that's mine.

I turn on music, loud.

I've got to get it together. Linden has to get it together. Fist in my chest. Hands squeezing tears from my eyes. I can't do this. I can't do this alone. I need to find my dad. I need to bring him home. So I can yell at him. Right in his face. Shake some sense into him.

I want to see Jess but her mom won't let me back in to see her. I saved her daughter and she won't let me back in. Drove me home not out of niceness, but to gain control again. Control she'd given up so easily just hours before. Where the hell had she been? What kind of mother is she? I can only imagine what it was like with her dad. His thick face, his blunt fingers, his accurate punches.

I'm walking a slow circle, trying to breathe. Trying to be calm. My phone beeps. I left it sitting on the counter all morning. Maybe it's Linden. Who cares. It's not enough. Could be my dad. Who cares. It's not enough.

Morse's door lazes against the wall. This old door, waterstained along the bottom. Her door, his door. The reason for all of this. Along the opposite wall there's a pile of locks, like a cache of balls just asking to be thrown. The music is loud and angry.

I throw lock after lock. They hit, take chips out of the wood and land on the floor. I put everything into the throws. My whole body, my whole back. I wind up, lift my front leg and I throw them past the plate, aiming through the door. Chips fly, locks land with a thwack, the air behind making the sound hollow; they land on the floor with a slower, softer, thud. One of my throws opens a crack, down near the bottom. Like a wrinkle, the scar on Jess's arm. I stop. This door that's survived so much can't take this either. Can't take me either.

I slide down the wall. There's no space for sense. There's no room for anything. This emptiness is totally full.

When she finally arrives, Linden's wearing yesterday's clothes. She's probably this late because she had to wait this long for her alcohol levels to drop before she could drive. I've cracked Mrs Morse's door and I feel pretty bad about that, but not as bad as I think I should feel. I am surrounded by corks and paper and thumbtacks. A glorious mess. My mess.

'Hey there, whore.'

Why should I beat around the bush?

'Watch your language Miss…' she stops. Surveys the wreckage. 'Oh my god, Roe. What have you done?'

'Me? What have I done? That's pretty special coming from you. But then maybe that's right, what have I done? We'll get to that. First let's start with what you didn't do. You didn't call, you didn't come home, you didn't think.'

'I…' she starts to protest. I put up a hand. Talk to the hand.

'But me. Let's see. I'm only fifteen so I can't be up to much, you think. Well you're wrong. Let's see… I was at Jess's house at five this morning after she barricaded herself in her room to protect her from her rampaging father, and then I went to the hospital in the ambulance, she's got loads of stitches, a broken wrist, blah blah blah. I've sat with Jess while the police interviewed her; I've sat with some sour faced lawyer while she took notes, and then I've come home to a still empty house. A message on the machine. You saying you'll be back 'sometime soon'. And then I have to go open Dad's shop and pretend anything is okay or normal. I only last fifteen minutes and I come home and it's still hours after that and you think that's good enough?'

She stares.

'And the house, well. Dad hasn't bothered his ass to come home yet so to hell with it, I might as well make it my own. He doesn't want it. He has to know that things have changed.'

She starts to walk over to me, but I don't let her near. She swerves towards the door like that's where she was heading all along, leans over and runs her finger along the crack. 'Oh, Roe. I'm so sorry. So sorry.'

His workspace looks broken, not as in smashed or unsteady, but as if it's lost its will. I see that. The damaged door. What sort of legacy is that?

She sits down at the kitchen table. Makes a pile of all the papers. Rubs her hands over the table. 'I'm sorry I didn't come home last night.'

This isn't your home, I want to yell. I know why you didn't come back. You don't want this responsibility. It's too much for you. I'm too much for you.

'I had some thinking to do.'

Is that what sex is called these days? I tap my fingers in a big-deal-you-had-a thought way.

'I went to see Frankie.'

Her best friend from high school, ex-cheerleader, law professor at the

University of Michigan, Frankie.

'She helped me sort through some things. There was lake effect snow on I-94, by Gary. An accident holding everything up. It was a nightmare, it took forever to get back. I left a message on your cell.'

Blah blah blah. What about me? What about the hospital? What about all these things that will never be okay again? I look at the clock. It's only three.

'I've cancelled my show.'

'What?'

'I've cancelled the exhibition.'

Her solo show. The one she's worked towards for years. The one she's been so busy with we've not seen her for six months before this thing started. I sit down. Sobered.

'You didn't have to do that.'

'Isn't it exactly what I needed to do? Isn't that what you're yelling at me about?'

She has a point.

'Finding Peter is too important. You're too important.' She doesn't do the meaningful look thing, for which I'm grateful. 'You need me here and, I need to be here. I miss Peter and I want the stupid man to come home. I can't be getting it ready and be here too. I've already called Robert.'

'How did he take it?'

'Doesn't matter.' She smiles and makes it true. 'Sounds like you've had a rough time. Is Jess okay?'

Rough week, rough who-knows-how-long to come. 'Yes, she'll be okay. She ended up flirting with the cop so I assume she's already on the mend.'

Linden keeps the conversation level, serious. She's not to be swayed into frivolity. Not today. 'Does she need anything?'

Yes. She needs a decent father. Don't we all. She needs a responsible mother. She needs a safe place to come home to.

'Can she come stay here with us when she's better?'

I'm only half joking.

'You'll have to ask your dad when he gets home. But she's welcome here anytime as long as I'm here and we can make it somewhat above board with her mom.'

We're sitting across the table from each other. This is serious stuff.

'I called my boss at the Art Institute to get some time off this week and really get to work to try and find Peter. He's got to be out there and I'll find him. Contact his old pals from out west, really apply myself.' She lifts all the scraps I've ripped from the corkboard. 'Will any of this be important?'

'Maybe.' At this point I don't have a clue about any of this. 'Can I help?'

'I think you need to go to school. If we're going to do this thing right, I'm going to have to obey state laws and all the rest of it. Including signing tests which may not show your brainy side in a good light.' She turns over a few menus, pizza, Chinese, Thai. 'An F minus is quite an achievement.'

So much for my secret. Keeping the hard stuff from her. 'How did you know about the test?'

'Oh come on, the erasing the messages on the machine trick? I've been picking them up remotely. To check for police messages. Your history debacle has been pure entertainment. What's happened now?'

'I switch classes from Monday. He kicked me out of class on Tuesday and then wouldn't let me back in on Thursday.'

'What happened to Wednesday?'

'I ditched school.'

'Ms Roe Davis. I didn't know you had it in you.'

'When he wouldn't let me back into class, despite the note, I called him a perv in front of the whole class.'

'Was that smart?'

'It was true.'

'Well, Monday should be an interesting day for you.'

'Don't I know it.'

From one thing to another, and Linden rolls with the punches.

We order pizza. 'Everything. We'd like everything on it,' she says into the phone.

Linden finds a tape of a game the Cubs actually won. July 2004. We're at the game. Dad stays at home, tapes it for us. We sit on the third base line. This is the team that will take us all the way: Sosa, Alou, Patterson, Ramirez, Maddux. He pitches a near perfect game. And the Cubs hit and hit and hit. A one-run homerun, a two-run homerun, a three-run, then a grand-slam. In order, like an ascending scale. A statistical thrill. And it's hotter than hell in the sun, but the clouds save us just enough. And there it is, there's a flash of us and our signs, I hold a sign that says, 'We're not Cubs', and Linden one that says, 'We're chicks who like Cubs'.

A perfect game. A perfect day. It's good to know they exist and that sometimes you can pull them out and replay them again and again.

'Should we start to clean this place up?'

'I suppose so.'

We empty some boxes and get some black bags. We watch two or three rather tacky movies back to back as we separate Mrs Morse's possessions: stuff for me, for dad, for charity, and stuff we've not decided about yet. It takes ages.

Her small knick-knacks. Letters tied with ripped silk, like the bottom hem of a dress. A baby book for Lauren. A funeral service for Mr Morse. Private things. I'm eavesdropping on her life. I keep things that look important, but don't read them yet. Linden deals with the neutral objects: clothes and sheets and napkins, all her pots and pans.

Short statements from Linden as she put more things in the 'to keep' box: 'Solid pressure cooker.' 'Feel the weight of this cast iron frying pan.'

At some point Linden parks her car on the street and I back dad's into the drive and we put the furniture where the car used to be.

'A bit more protected anyway.'

The garage's mess is too much to even contemplate dealing with.

Linden does the dishes which have piled up in the sink. Then she tries to find something for a snack.

'These cupboards are bare, Ms Roe.'

'And no wonder, you eat like a horse, Linden.'

She's opening and closing cabinets, the fridge. 'Some cabbage?'

'My own stomach lining?'

'How about tea and cookies?'

'Sounds good.'

She puts water in the kettle and puts it on the stove. I clean off the table and wipe it clear with my sleeve. I sit down and flip through Mrs Morse's old *National Geographic* magazines. She had a full set all the way back to the '60s. Neatly lined up in boxes. Linden leans against the counter.

'You know Roe, nothing has to change,' she says.

I laugh. Of course it does. It already has. She smiles. She doesn't know all the things I know, I don't know all the things she knows, but it's clear we share an elastic sense of reality.

There's been something nagging at me. All these similarities. All these things about me that are so Davis. Nature vs nurture and all that but isn't there a possibility that my mother knew I'd be tall? That she feels the free-spirit Davis blood mixing with her own? And my stubborn streak a mile wide, my heels shoved into her ribs, in utero, sealing the deal. Me insisting she remembers who'd made me. That she remembers whose daughter I am.

Not yours. His. His. His. His. His.

She grabs my heel. 'Peter's daughter. I know. I know.'

And she seeks him out. Reads him like a book. Forces his hand while making him feel that he has free will. She knows him. Knows exactly how to get him to take some responsibility.

'Don't you think it's strange that I ended up with you giants?' I ask Linden.

'Not at all. It was fate. Pure and simple.'

'Fate? Or a carefully organized drop?' She raises an eyebrow. I've piqued her interest, truth and beauty. 'Linden, who's my dad?'

She doesn't blink, doesn't fidget. 'I don't know.'

'Could you give an educated guess?'

'I could guess. I'm not sure what would be educated about it.'

'Could it be dad? Peter?'

'He's never talked about it.' She steps forward and pushes my hair off my forehead to the side and smoothes it down. Then she weighs my face in both her hands.

I need this. I know I need this.

'I think you're his. I think you're a Davis.'

My off-center grin, my sexual indiscretions, my tells.

'What does dad think?'

The kettle's whistle goes. She steps away, fills our mugs with hot water. Places chocolate chip cookies on the table between us. Meets my eyes, smiles full and warm, as honest as honest can be.

'How can he not know you're his?'

Exactly.

When I go to bed I see that she's picked up my mess, put all the locks back on dad's workspace, wiped the door with a cloth, gathered the splinters. Cleaned the floor. Exhaustion sweeps down my body. In bed the dark is close, the wind hitting the house, buffeting it.

I'm four or so, my dad and I are at Marshall Field's downtown, after visiting some antique shops. He's there. I'm there. Suddenly I'm gone or he's gone or whatever and we are no longer together. Tight like hands round my ribs. I'm desperate. My whole world collapses. It's not about to collapse, it's already gone. I'll never find him again. He'll never find me. Up and down the aisles. It takes about a minute for me to be hysterical. And about ten seconds for some sales assistant to squat down, ask me my name.

'Roe,' I say.

'What a pretty name,' she says, but what she really means is, *Who'd do that to a kid. What a name.* Her hair is parted, thick black strands. 'Who are you looking for?'

'My dad,' I say, tears, gasping, pulling down on my skirt. 'My dad.'

She walks me to a sales desk. Over the intercom, 'Would Roe's dad please come to the Ladies' Lingerie department?'

Seconds are long. Long. I love the dress I have on. A calico sundress. And he's never coming back, never.

And then he shows up. Calm as anything. 'There you are.' Like we're playing hide and seek. Doesn't he know, doesn't he know? I gasp and splutter. And he holds me, holds me until I stop crying. It's a long time before I stop.

That night he reads me one story as usual. Gives me a quick hug, a light kiss on the cheek and turns off the light. Like always.

SUNDAY

I'm awake instantly. The phone ringing. My heart jumping out of my chest. Racing. Asleep and calm and then awake and shaking.

My heart flutters. Who calls this early on a Sunday?

I reach over to answer it; I see the clock, 11:45, quite a reasonable hour actually. My hand shakes slightly.

'Hello?'

'Roe?'

A male voice. Not my dad. Not my dad.

'This is Duncan.'

The dud. Too early for this. Any time is too early for this. Linden's come to the door.

'Hi, Duncan.'

She makes hand signals that she's not here.

He clears his throat. I can almost see him brushing out wrinkles in his shirt. Making himself presentable. 'Mel and I were thinking of popping in this afternoon. She thought we should phone first.'

Duh. Of course you should. Pros of a visit: nil. Cons: the list is long.

'I think it'd be best if you didn't come over today. The house is a mess with all of Mrs Morse's stuff over here.'

'Why is it over at your house?'

His voice harsh. Cutting. How could you be so stupid as to move her stuff? He doesn't know.

'Didn't Linden phone you? Tell you?'

'Tell us what?'

'The Village tore her house down on Friday.'

'It's a listed building, they can't do that.'

'It is? Was?'

'That's how Peter saved it last year. He asked me how to go about it.'

We should have phoned Duncan on Thursday. I never thought about that.

'Well, it's gone now. They quoted public safety infringements, building code violations. They only told us on Thursday at 5:00 p.m.'

'I'm sorry, Roe.'

'Anyway. It's a mess and we're spending the day sorting it. My dad would be shocked if he walked into this.'

'I'm sure he'd adapt; but we understand. Is Linden there?'

'She's still asleep.'

So he'll try to bully her into having them come over so he can snoop.

'How's she doing?'

Genuine concern. Didn't know he had it in him.

'Um. Fine. Tired. She's cancelled her show, so she can try to find dad.'

Empty space. Nothing. Him trying to figure out how he can muscle in and take over the efforts.

'Wow. She cancelled her exhibition? That's huge. She must be devastated.' I hadn't thought. 'Have her phone me when she gets up. It'd be good to talk to her.'

He's gone all soft. Nice. Duncan, is it you Duncan? Where's the real Duncan?

'Say hi to Mel.'

'Will do. See you soon?'

'Yes. We'll phone.'

'We're looking forward to it.'

I hang up. Exhale. Rub my face. Put my hair behind my ears. I hate unexpected phone calls, those early morning crank calls, I always expect it'll be something bad.

Just Duncan. Just Duncan.

'Thanks for swerving him off my scent. I wasn't ready for him yet.'

'He was okay actually. Nice even.'

'Duncan?'

'My heart's still pounding with the phone ringing like that.'

'Mine too. Coffee?'

'You read my mind. Should we make some breakfast too? Plan for the day?'

'How about waffles?' she asks, laughing.

'You've got to be kidding.'

'I'll go to the store and get what we need for omelets.'

'Peppers, mushrooms and cheese?'

'Potatoes too, for hash browns.'

'Perfect.'

I pull on a robe, slip into my spaceship slippers and go downstairs. Linden gets dressed and then comes down. She stands beside me. Gives me a quick hug. Cold cheeks, smoke in her hair, the smell of exhaustion.

There's no use waiting for things to get better by themselves. That's not the way it usually works. You've got to make them better. Save them.

She's going to go through his papers, call whoever seems like a good bet. I'm going to continue to go through Mrs Morse's things. Do some homework for school tomorrow. Answer any questions she has. I put the brunch dishes in the sink.

'You know that box you were talking about?'

The delicate box, with its equally delicate mate, both waiting under my bed.

'Yes.'

'Do you think you could?'

'Open it?'

'If you felt you could.'

My fingers have been itching to do it since we started talking. We've turned a corner, we're officially worried. We're changing the terms to our terms. And all these small things might point us in the right direction, might be important.

He'll come home regardless of whether or not I open the box.

Or not.

'I'm going to do his hope chest first.'

'Great idea,' says Linden. She's not going to look into anything without conferring with me first. Or letting me do it first.

The hope chest is full to bursting.

That broken padlock. My dad the sentimentalist.

Baseball cards, one ancient block of bubblegum.

High school report cards.

Newspaper clippings about Mrs Morse's being taken by the lake. Photos of waves biting into house. A picture of Mrs Morse standing at the edge of the ravine, looking down, after the storm. She looks old.

A scrawled note confirming that he rode the Class 5 rapids on the Colorado, signed by someone named Butch.

Papers about his apprenticeship as a locksmith out in New Mexico. Mr Taylor, master craftsman. A letter of recommendation too.

The loan grandpa gave him when he first bought the shop.

It's all dad here. All dad.

I shout for Linden to come up and have a look.

'Lots in here. Not much that will help.' She smiles and sits on the floor. 'That box there,' I point to the laden boxfile where I had tried to find the lawyer's number, 'might have some helpful stuff in it. May the goddess of patience be with you. I've left it unlocked.'

I go to my room and take out the delicate boxes. I pile my dad's on top of Mrs Morse's, which is slightly wider, and carry them downstairs so that I'll have space to have a good look at them.

'Let me know if you find anything,' Linden says from within dad's bedroom.

'Will do.'

I clear off my dad's worktop. Place Mrs Morse's box and my dad's box side by side.

They're both light but, unlike before when I thought they were empty, now I'm not so sure. They're bottom heavy, and both make a small sound like shifting sands when I move them from side to side.

Unusually for my dad, neither box has a key hanging from the side (and no hook where it should be) and both are locked. To most people, but not me. It's my dad's design, I twist my hair back and put it up out of my face, off my neck. I lift my dad's box, run my hands over all sides, three straight, one curving out. The squared bit of the box is just bigger than a sheet of notebook paper. The knot curves, stretches out beyond this. There's paper in here. Mrs Morse's box is the same, full sized, wider than the other one, with the curve inwards still allowing for a full rectangle shape within the box.

I reach for a small pick and close my eyes. I imagine my dad, things he wants to keep safe, but not secret. Not from me anyway. He wants me to be able to find things when I'm ready. The lock takes a soft touch. I know this system. It's not open to everyone, but it's open to me.

When I feel the lock on my dad's box give a click, I slide a thin card between the lid and the side of the box. And then I release Mrs Morse's lock. They're not identical, they're mirrors or joined in someway. I imagine that their keys would fit together like hands, or bodies.

I flip both boxes open in quick succession. Don't trust my eyes. They're empty. Locked and empty. My dad the joker. The joke's on me. The biggest clues are missing. The things he thought I should wait for, and there's nothing there.

I stand up to my full height, open my hands and put one in each box. With my fingers I follow the edges to one corner and then the next and then the next, I slide around the curves, my hands so close they could be clasped, and then apart again around the final corner.

Nothing. Nothing.

I take my dad's box. It seems deeper on the outside than on the inside. I pick it up and shake it again and again. The smallest, quietest movement inside. I click on my dad's spotlight, his work light. Pull over his stool. Put my feet up on the bars.

Linden's come downstairs, carrying a big pile of papers. And then she turns on the stereo.

'This okay?' she asks.

'Fine,' I shout back.

I turn the box around and flip it over. All the joints are perfectly smooth. I search for a ruler and measure the dimensions. The thickness of the wood. I discount the curves and measure from the corners. By my calculations there's half an inch extra at the bottom. On the side with the lock, there's a small anomaly, barely enough to consider, except we're dealing with my dad and his craft. This is the sort of thing he loves.

I look closely at the lock. If I had a magnifying glass, I'd use that. At the bottom corner on the wide front, there's a hole the size of a needle's point, a hairsbreadth.

I look through my dad's drawers. Nothing that's the right size.

He'd want me to be able to do this in one sitting, right here. I look at the box again. Integral to the lock, at the back, where it's attached to the inside of the box, there's a small hole, which looks to run the length of the body of the lock. With my fingernails I pinch and pull out a small thin pin. Once I catch it, it slides out smooth.

Mrs Morse's lock will look exactly the same. I leave it for later. It's his secrets I want to know.

I stare at my dad's open, empty box. Run my fingers along the bottom. The false bottom. The assumption that I already knew everything I needed to know.

I push the point of the pin into the hole. I hear a lever slide and push. The bottom pops up. I inhale but it sounds like a gasp.

Not a sound from Linden. She's good. Really good. I'd have been over in a flash.

There's no note of explanation. I'm not meant to open these things yet. He expected to be there with me when I opened this box.

On the top there's a photo of my mom. Not holding me, but by a cliff of rock, in her climbing gear. In her element. My dad right there too. In his bare feet. Does he look at home? Does he look in love? I can't tell. And there's another of her holding me as a baby, out back of the house. Mel's rosemary growing wild behind her. The wind strong, I'm wrapped up warm. It must be spring but it doesn't look like it yet.

Beneath the photos is my birth certificate. Mother: Chris Melissa Cartright. Baby's name: Roe Catriona Cartright. 7lbs 8 ozs. 20 inches long. No father's name. No answers.

Her death certificate. I was only two years old.

Her will and the adoption papers, including my official change of name. Roe Bryn Cartright Davis.

A letter from Mrs Morse to my dad. Marked by a notary public, the seal, waxed with her small metal insignia which is now downstairs in the 'to keep' box, broken, the bits of wax in the envelope with the letter. *My Dearest Peter*, the letter starts, and somehow I don't want to read any more. What was her first name? I flip through the pages, *sorry, house, door*, words I spot. *Love, Sarah*. The letter ends. I fold the paper and put it back in the envelope.

Things I'm not meant to know until I'm older. He's supposed to pull this box out, run his hands over the top to disperse the dust and he's supposed to hand this box to me and go over and sit at the kitchen table, drinking a cup of coffee or a small glass of bourbon, pretending to read or do a crossword while I try to work this conundrum out. I hear him laughing under his breath.

'Discover anything, Roe?' Linden asks from the doorway.

'Yes, but nothing that's helpful to us today.'

'Want to talk about it?' She doesn't move closer, just turns down the music, yells around the corner.

'Later, maybe. Not just now. What have you found out?'

'Steve finally called back. Says they talked about getting away this summer.'

Steve, my dad's best friend since forever.

'He said that Peter talked about going to Alaska or Scotland or New Zealand. He says Peter thought you were old enough to stay home on your own. He was going to bring it up with you after your birthday.'

Three weeks away. He couldn't wait three weeks?

'Steve is on his way over. I've made a few other calls, no one else has heard anything. Knows anything. Most people didn't know he was gone.' She rubs her face. 'Lots of well-wishes and love to you,' she says. 'People keeping their eyes and ears open.'

The truth is well and truly out there. I'd like it if it were a bit closer to hand.

'Hey there, Linden.'

'Steve.'

They hug. It's a long hug. Then he hugs me; it's the same, strong and comforting.

Linden gets us glasses of water, he can't stay long.

'It wasn't really a fight,' Steve says. 'I thought he should wait until Roe went to college. He thought that was unrealistic. That she could handle it just fine if he took some time this summer. I thought he was being a bit selfish.'

Did my dad ever escape to go out drinking with Steve? Hang out at his apartment downtown for days at a time? Did he tell Steve that he'd left me at home, at the mercy of Linden's and Mel's kindness? Does Steve know this now? Did he know this before?

I hardly ever get to see Steve. It's like my dad keeps him separate, like an escape. I'm really liking him. He's beautiful. Far sexier than my dad, who is tall and dark but too gangly to be handsome. They must pull lots of women when they're out on the town.

'Do you think he accepted what you said?' Linden asks.

'I did, until you phoned. Now I'm not sure. I know there were a lot of things going on in his head. The shop was doing well, but eventually he wanted to take on an apprentice or chuck it in altogether.'

My dad giving up the shop?

'I have to say though, he always talked about stuff like that much further in the future. Once Roe had left home. As a next stage. It felt like he was testing the waters with me, as to how you guys would react.'

Not well. We would not react very well.

'Could he have been playing down how important it was to him?' Linden asks.

'Yes,' Steve says. 'That's all I've been thinking about. That I thought it was light-hearted. A bit of a whim. And he was desperate, really needed me to do something. Question him. Support him.' He turns to me. 'I'm sorry, Roe. I'm sorry I can't give you more. That I didn't stop him.'

'None of us did, could have.'

'He's always been a bit of a wiley coyote,' Steve says. He stands up. 'Sorry it's a running visit. I've got a mother to go see. I'll let you know if I hear anything.'

'Would love some of that,' Linden says as we watch him put his gorgeous body into his car.

'Focus Linden. Focus.'

'I am. I mean, I will.'

I go for a run. The air is turning warmer, still cold, just not quite so bitter. I look forward to this snow shifting and new snow falling, clean and white. I'm on the home-stretch, just taking our front stairs two at a time when I hear my name.

'Roe!'

I turn around and Mr Taylor is coming down his stairs and across the street to meet me. He hands me a memory card from a camera, 'I took pictures when they tore the house down. Don't know, thought you might want a record of it. When you sue them.'

I look up. If he hadn't come out of their house I'm not sure I'd recognize him. They've got a son who's two years older than me. I can't remember his name. He's a bit of a geek.

'It should work on any computer. Any problems ring the bell and I can help you out.'

'Thanks.' My head is empty. Strangers feel like they have to help me out. How pathetic am I? How helpless do I look? 'I'll get the card back to you soon.'

'Take your time. If there's anything else Roe, let me know. We're praying for you and Peter.'

Praying for us. In people's thoughts and prayers.

I was doing fine before this. And now I'm a victim, someone who needs to be cared for. Before I was just Roe. Roe Davis. Slightly tall for her age, average in school, good at science, exciting to watch play baseball. Adopted, but people have more or less forgotten that, if they ever knew it. I'm not sure Jess really knows much about it. But now, abandoned. It's a label that'll stick. Damn him.

Linden's car is gone, a note on the table, 'I forgot to get milk.'

The answerphone blinks. I let it play as I take off my shoes and I circle one foot, and then the other, at the ankle.

Peter? This is Alan Kauffman. I've been trying you at work and on your cell all week. I finally found your home number. I hope I have the dates wrong and there's still time, or you did something to delay the Village's actions. Call me ASAP and we'll sort it. We have some strong options. We'll be able to save the house.

Off come the socks and my sweater. My lovely sweater. Boxy, black, all me. My toes curl. It's a wood floor and the boards are rough sanded, the stain slapdashed. I've created just enough space for the movement I'll create.

I am long, my center, a line of vertebrae, bound by muscles. I flip the yoga mat out and lay it down. Then I lie down. I stretch.

We could have saved it. We could have saved Morse's house.

MONDAY

Linden is up and has poured orange juice into a glass for me. That's as far as she's gone.

'I have no idea what you eat before breakfast.'

'Orange juice is a good start.' I take a sip and put a bagel in the toaster.

'I've written you a note for your absence on Friday.' She's smiling. 'Want to hear it?'

Dear Mrs Homeroom Teacher,

My niece Roe missed school on Friday because the Village decided it had the right to demolish her next door neighbor's house. Her father, who is missing, actually owns this property. I'm sure you are aware of his absence and I'd like you to cut her some slack. Stop pushing her to apologize to the bullying history teacher. She has nothing to apologize for.

Sincerely,
Linden Bryn Davis
(her aunt, who has no legal authority whatsoever, but will have to do given the circumstances)

I put cream cheese and some lox on the bagel and stick it in a bag to eat during homeroom.

'Running late. See you tonight. Thanks for the note.'

'Don't go getting kicked out of any classes, you hear. You've got the Davis reputation to uphold.'

She winks. Nothing like a parent at all. I'll take what I can get.

Mrs Warner reads the note as soon as I hand it to her. I should play it safe, soft, but I don't. I play it neutral. I go to my seat and answer Tina's questions about my dad, calmly, in between bites of my bagel.

'Don't know.' 'Nothing's changed.' 'No idea.'

'Roe,' Mrs Positive Thinking says, 'can I see you out in the hall?'

I roll my eyes at Tina. Take my breakfast with me.

'How are you?' She creases her brow, puts her hand on my forearm.

'I'm fine,' I say.

'Is this, ehm, this *Linden*,' she slows down, reads it out phonetically, 'really your aunt?'

'No, she's my dog.' She looks up. Alarmed. Sense of humor bypass. 'Of course she's my aunt.'

'Well then, you may go back inside. And you should really apologize to Mr Pavich.' Same old dog, same old bone. 'You don't want that bad-will out there to bite back later.'

I'll say it until I'm blue in the face. 'I don't have anything to apologize for.'

I see her through the window of the door, holding her head. Shaking it. Poor Roe Davis, she thinks, I'll think some good thoughts on her behalf because her sarcasm will not serve her well.

It'll serve me better than her stupid false spineless goodwill.

Gym sucks. Always has, always will. We're into the second week of retro, girly inside activities. Climbing ropes, and doing chin-ups on these flip down ladders. I know when I tell Linden about it, she'll remember it. The equipment looks decades old. The gym teacher makes us do hamburger sprints for forever. But it's meek and too short to get up a good sweat. Just enough to be sticky. I am missing how I am in my body. The freedom of baseball, the concentration.

Coach Feldman is at the door and greets me as I go past. 'Looking a bit rusty, Roe. You should be training.'

'I know. I'll start next week.'

'You should start today. The thaw's here, you'll be able to get up to speed. You should be thinking about college scholarships. There are some great girls' teams out there. Come in after school and do circuits. Start training with the track team.'

Scholarships? College? That's not today or tomorrow but years away. There's something great about the fact that it's years away, waiting for me.

'I did some matwork yesterday.'

'Good, Roe. Core work is important.'

My powerhouse. Mine. 'I'll try to get to training this week.'

'I know it's a tough time for you. Sometimes routine helps us through. Passes the time too. Makes you strong.'

'Back to the basics,' Mr R says. 'We're going to start a new project today. I want you to record a story for me. It can be through pictures, film, sound or writing. I don't want you to bust through the story like a bull in a china shop. I want you to find your way in, your way of telling it.

'First I want you to listen to the soundscapes which provide background to what we live. These things we hear, or see, which help build up the whole picture.' He presses a button. There's birdsong. There's a car's horn. Distant voices. He continues talking, 'These happen behind the immediate scene. The interactions we have with the outside world: people, landscapes, objects. Voices, in particular, the words, then the meaning, provide a rich source of lived and shared material.' On the tape a man and a woman are arguing, he's dismissive and she's sarcastic. It escalates and escalates until Mr R flicks off the tape. 'Things are communicated in thousands of ways. For sound, the intonation, the volume, the pace, and the sincerity of the voice that speaks is important.'

'Great!' he says, all enthusiasm.

'Great,' he says, deadpan, the height of sarcasm.

'Visually, body language does the same thing. It can be quite important to listen to what is going on at the same time as the words, what is behind the words, what's between the words. What is 'other' gives the words even more significance, or even a different meaning altogether. A glance, a physical clue.'

Tells. I know all about these. I know his. Even without his beard, Mr R's thinking hard when he rubs his thumb on the side of his face. And when he's at ease, he's like this, exuberant.

'Ask yourself about how alive you are. About what you notice and what passes you by. As you start to think how you want to tell a story, listen to how other people express theirs. Did you know that when some painters paint the sky, they often put other colors, usually red, beneath the blue of the sky? It gives the skyscape depth, perspective. What are the colors of your life? Or the soundtracks? What will define your life when you look back?'

I look up. His neatly shaved jawline, his wedding ring still gone, but the line less clear.

'You should remember these days,' he says, 'they're important. As you think about this assignment think about what stories you would tell about these days; what facts would you want to record? What sounds? What images? What layers? How would you tell your own story?'

So an easy assignment then?

The cafeteria is packed. I'm yesterday's news. I've been trying to get a hold of Quiz all day. He's not answered his phone all weekend; Mrs Berg took messages but he's not phoned back. I spot him and slide onto a bench across from him. Our trays between us.

'Get up and walk away, Roe. I don't want to eat with you. Don't want to see you.'

'Quiz, you're over-reacting.'

'Really? Really? Is that what I'm doing?'

'Yes.'

'You kiss Jason, Jason Park, of all people, in front of the entire school, necking for "like an hour" is what Colin told me.'

Colin who?

'And you think I'll just take it, act like it never happened...'

When he puts it like that.

He slams both hands, palm down, on the table. My chocolate pudding quavers. My peas jump.

'Roe. You're taking after Jess and that's not a good thing.'

'Stay focused, Quiz. Don't drag Jess into this. You don't want to do that.'

I get up. There's having insight and there's going too far. He stands with me, grabs my arm.

'No wonder he left, Roe. No wonder he left you. Really, who'd have you?'

I'm sure the whole room has heard him. I'm sure the whole room has seen just how right he is. But there are hundreds of dramas being lived all around us. Hardly anyone bats an eyelid. There's nothing I can say. There's truth that's known and truth that's lived. This is both.

'Let go, Quiz.'

But he hesitates that second too long. He wants a scene? He wants rude? I raise my voice. I speak clearly.

'Fuck you, Mr I've-just-got-all-the-piercings-in-the-world and I-think-I'm-cool-Berg. Fuck you, I-can't-be-bothered-to-act-like-a-decent-human-being-Berg. Fuck you.'

My exit is neither smooth nor clumsy. It just is. Like flat ginger ale. No oomph. No kick.

In the bathroom, after bells have signaled the end and the beginning of classes, when all the low voices in the bathroom have gone, when I can hear each drip in the sink from a loose washer, when it's empty, I sit. It smells like bleach and overly sweet perfume and acrid hairspray. And I sit.

Over the intercom I get called to the principal's office.

The secretary tells me Linden's on her way to pick me up and that I can wait outside on the chair. It's the same thing as telling me he's dead. If he was here, he'd be here. If he'd been found somewhere else, she'd phone me or text me, 'We've found him,' and let me get on with my day. Because that'd be no big news, just a return to normal, perfect.

I don't know how he's dead or where he's dead. Just that he is. From inside the office I hear the secretary on the phone, 'ice' and 'fallen', and that's all I need.

This is how it played. A silent movie. A farce.

He has never been able to run well, not even as a child. He's all legs. He settles right into a saunter though. His first cowboy boots, his bare feet.

His work, his hobbies. The years he spends away. The women. Then he comes home. He walks. He sits on a plane. He should have run. Nearly too late.

He gets to his dad, just in time. Spends a few months with him, gives him his love. He's there for his dad in his failing health, to make up for the mom whose death he missed.

During summer he gets so hot he burns up, rods of fire for a skeleton. He loves that feeling. Autumn oscillates between the two and just passes him by without notice, but winter, now that wakes him up, clear as a bell. Ice to the shore, like metal to wood, the perfect complements.

And the cold bites like heat. Through his jeans, his gloves, at the part of his face that's exposed, and he doesn't miss a single moment of the day. He's at his most clear. The long dark of winter, so very very compelling.

I come to him in winter during a March cold snap and my mom unwraps me in his shop, like a gift, my face red and hot and my legs fighting the blanket. When he holds me, he lets it fall open, and my legs are free and in the air I am calm. Clear. There is something familiar about those legs and he wants to take me home. Not just any child, but me. And providence is with him. And with me.

It's a Friday night in January. We sit at the table. I'm picking my nose and he's picking a lock. I'm thinking about having sex with Quiz; I don't know what he's thinking but I'm guessing it has something to do with tomorrow or the day after. Or the day after that. I do know that he's not thinking that he's a clumsy runner or that it'll be his downfall. I know that even if he's struggling with being my dad, he's not going to stumble. Not going to abandon me willingly.

I sit and watch him. He works the lock. He's all concentration and when he hugs me good night his hug is simple, everyday.

It's freezing. I'm safe asleep in the house. Our haven. The wind cuts his legs and they're cold now, bitter with the windchill, he thinks about how they will be hot later, inside, prickly with the warming up. The ice has built up, like he's never seen it before. Great flat pieces swing against each other. The water is dark under the thin moon. The thinnest sliver of a moon and yet it's still bright. Snow falls, and it's magical. The ravine is steep, exposed and protects him and the beach from the worst of the wind. Mrs Morse's house at the edge smiles over and he's not sure he'll be able to save it this time. He couldn't save her. Or her daughter. Or her husband.

The world is bright. He thinks he'll talk to me about his need to travel. About me staying with Linden this summer. He thinks I'm old enough. Almost sixteen. What's the worst thing that can happen? It changes my view of my old man?

There's no wind, no cracks of ice, no water slushing, not close in or further out, only his breath. His mind clear of thoughts. He has an urge to flight. He will look like a fool but there's no one here to see him. He stuffs his notes and his wallet into the roots of a tree. And he runs, gangly frog legs, open arms. Like he read in a book once. He runs on the ice of the lake, parallel to the shore. It's dark but the ice is solid. And he runs. How can he not run?

And he knows as his right foot meets nothing solid that he has made a horrible, deadly miscalculation.

He has fallen. He will not be found until the first thaw.

He has been found by a skinny jogger who trips over his forearm which is sticking straight up through ice that's been pushed onto the frozen sand by a winter storm just that morning. The chunks that conceal his body sawing against the shore. The police have to get in quick before the day, a scorcher in the fifties, heats everything up. The world melting. Corpses bloating.

And the boys were just rough-housing as usual in the ravines. Wanting to go out on the ice, but not quite having the guts. They'd found strange things down on the beach before: a whole unfettered raft, *The Thomsons of the UP* screenprinted on the side, loosed from its mooring and floated all the way here from Northern Michigan. They broke it up for firewood, hid it in the ravines. A Canadian goose with its neck broken, maggots in its eyes. A brand new bike with a pink ribbon still tied to the handlebars. And a wedding ring, tossed, they imagined in a rage from the top.

'Fuck you Miles Lawson!' A call I'd heard one night. 'And fuck you Catriona Schwartz!' Added with fervor, disappointment.

The boys didn't think it was strange to find a wallet and a duffle bag with some maniac's scribbled notes. And once they'd grabbed them and used the paper for kindling, and the money for booze, and the cards for gas to visit a friend at U of I, knowing full well who he was, and once he'd been declared missing, how could they admit to it?

That's okay with me. I see that. But how could Jason kiss me, knowing my dad might be dead?

Linden holds my hand. We've been told he might not be recognizable. He's on a slab, a table, whatever. It's not like he just drowned, he's been frozen too. He's bruised, battered by the ice, a slice of his cheek taken out which they've tried to hide by turning his head to his side. Away from us.

I move forward but Linden hangs back. Our arms stretch. I pull her with me. Be the adult. Be strong for me. Please. This is about me. It only takes a small tug and then she's there too. Looking at my dad. Her brother. I touch his hair, his face. It's disgusting. But I touch him anyway. Put my hand on his chest, an action I'd never have done if he was alive. His hands are just flesh over bones. His gangly legs poke the sheet up: his toes, his knees, his hip bones. It's a law, I think. That the easiest answer is usually right. He was clumsy, too adventurous for his own skill, and he fell. The treachery of ice. His papers and wallet in the roots of a tree, safely on shore when his body was trapped down there, under ice that wouldn't budge. Couldn't melt.

Half a mile from home this whole time. I lean over and whisper in his ear.

'They bulldozed Mrs Morse's house. I couldn't stop them.'

Linden's hand in mine. Squeezing.

'Yes, it's him,' she says to the officer.

When I see him, the crisp sound of the metal drawer, there's only Linden's breath and mine and the muffled rustle of the white sheets over his body. And his voice, in my ear, Mrs Morse's too. These conversations, these lost conversations.

'And she was the love of my life,' he says, 'you've never seen such a beautiful girl. Not until you came along. You were the most beautiful baby. You are the most beautiful girl. My most beautiful girl.'

Mrs Morse has her hands resting one over the other on her lap, until she stretches one out and touches my knee. 'You should have seen her. All the good in the world. Everything was hers. This is what she brought; this is what you bring, Roe. Don't forget you can't save everything.'

Linden drives slowly. Everything is melting and dripping. The world looks grey and muddy and dull. The snow flattens in the above zero heat and pocks like acne. The sky is low and threatening rain. By tomorrow everything will be free of snow, the world will be the color of cement.

We drive by the Indian Trail trees and they point us in the direction of the lake, of home. She's biting off bits of her dried lips and then pulling at them with her fingers. Her eyes are thin and watery and rimmed red with crying.

How can you not cry? He's gone. My doppling, my awkward, my clumsy dad is gone. My dad who was big and stubborn and unafraid. Restless, maybe. And now he's tragic too. A bit stupid. And that's a label that'll stick.

My dad loves me unconditionally all the way to the end and it doesn't matter. Dulled, like from inside a drum, my heart pounds on the skin, bursts at its limits.

Duncan and Mel are waiting in their car outside the house. Staring at the place Mrs Morse used to live, glancing in the rearview mirror, waiting for us to arrive. They know there's a key under the rock by the clump of hibernating chives. They're waiting out of respect. As we pull up, Mel gets out of the car to greet us. She opens my door, pours me out and into her arms.

'I'm so sorry, Roe. I'm so sorry.'

She holds me, her breath smells of mint leaves, her collar of exhaust and Duncan's cologne. I want to walk on my own but my legs don't seem to be working. My chest is sharp pins with each attempted breath. I am alive. Jab. I am alive. Jab. My head is heavy and absent. She clutches dried herbs in her hand. The bouquet is like smelling salts.

Linden gives Duncan the keys. And he opens the door like it's a stranger's house, without owning it at all. My feet are heavy but they won't hold me up. That's clear. They're blocks of bricks. Lead. They're there and Mrs Morse's house isn't and they can't help me clean up the mess. Mel and I step through. Duncan kisses me on the head as I pass by. His breath is hot and full. Linden and him follow us inside.

Duncan is visibly shaken. His hands show how upset he is as he does the crossword and Sudoku. Order order. Sense.

He touches nothing. *Leave only footprints.*

I remember one Thanksgiving when he explained to me how to restore the bindings of old books, about glue and pressure. I didn't really hear anything he said. I was mesmerized by the smooth action of his wrists, how delicately he held the paper, the spine. The resemblance is so clear. The future of so much depending on how careful he is with his hands.

And I'm glad he's here, finally being careful with the memory of dad.

It hurts. I hurt. This is what I will remember. How absence is nothing like perfection. How it has a presence like a punch, like a stabbing, like a gunshot. How it burns, in my chest, at my eyes, behind my forehead. How the house is too small, how I can't see. Can't hear. How warped the world is.

We talk. I don't know. It must matter but I just can't think how. I go up to my room. They're downstairs. Voices. They'll be talking about funerals and flowers and autopsies and wills and maybe even who'll be my guardian.

Please let it be Linden. Please let it be Linden.

I sit on my bed. I open Mrs Morse's box.

There's a birth certificate for Lauren. A picture Lauren must have drawn in first grade or something of a house with a curl of smoke, a round doorknob, shiny and black. A smiling trio standing in front, the lake blue and endless behind. Death certificates for both Mr Morse (Thomas) and Lauren. The original deed for the land on which the house was built. Mr Watson's hand-drawn plans for the old bit of the house. An architect's plans for the front section of the house, folded over and over to fit into the box. And a single, beautiful key. I know it won't fit, but I love the idea that it might. That she left it behind for my dad, or me.

There's no difference between crying and not crying. The feeling's the same. One's just wetter.

There's noise outside.

'Roe! Roe! Roe!'

And then a racket on the stairs. Jess hasn't phoned first and she doesn't knock on my door. She swings it open and is through in a flash, still with the hospital band around her wrist. Limping, a bit of blood seeping through the bandage on her face. And none of it matters. She only sees me. She sits beside me and gives me the strongest hug ever. She's crying for me.

'This sucks,' she says.

That just about sums it up.

Her phone rings, it's her mom. Jess is AWOL. But I know where she is. She's here for me.

And one day soon we'll laugh about the absurdity of it all. How can you not laugh? About how big he was, how true, how frustrating. And Duncan will laugh about being locked in the basement because it's classic Peter; him and Linden in hysterics about the smooshed Snickers or was it a Three Musketeers, and how she was too young for Peter to be really mean, except for how he used to hold her upside down and she'd punch at his legs 'feebly' she'll say, but how he took advantage of her kindness by waking her up with pebbles to the window so she could come downstairs and open the door after he'd been out drinking with Steve or Jude or any of his friends. And how he'd give her the ticket from the boat ride to Dime Pier, or a beer mat, or a button from the concert he hadn't been allowed to go to.

Mel will cook us a big dinner and Duncan will become known for picking the lock on the Russian Box, Take Me Out to the Ball Game bursting through the conversation, sudden, like dad's laugh. And he'll start bringing me small things that pass through the archive, 'Which are of little value,' he stresses, old Cubs pins and hats, long keys with designs similar to the ones on the door. Small things. And together we fix the door, just a little.

When Dad visits me in my dreams he says, Hi Roe. And I say, Hi Dad. Miss you my deer. Me too, I say. And he looks at me with those eyes, the eyes I share, which give everything, and absolutely nothing away.

At night Jess is often beside me, she's lost her dad too. Linden's asleep next door. Mel and Duncan sleep on the pullout bed of the couch when they stay over. There are boys down at the beach bragging, talking about a ring, a bike, a bird, the wallet of a dead man.

I'm running. And the sky is blue blue blue above our house. The lake is high and rising. The place where Mrs Morse's house used to be is a summer field of grasses and wildflowers. Me and Mel till it, and then I stand in the middle, turning and turning and letting the seeds fly and find homes. April showers bring May flowers. I'm keeping pace with everything. Everyone.

In this house by the water there's a magic door without a key mounted in our living room. It will never have a key. And it's unlocked, as it should be. Its hinges are the point of an arc and it takes an extra tug to pull it secure.

A door is a door is a door is an entrance, an exit, a portal, an heirloom, an excuse and a reason. And when you close a door you are making a decision to stay or to go.

Acknowledgements

A generous thank you goes to my family and friends and to the writers I have been lucky enough to work beside and to teach with over the years. Particular thanks goes to ARTT, for everything; and to the Denny/Boyd-Wallis family, for their friendship and for providing the perfect writing space for many summers running. Throughout the writing of this book I had one particular, superb reader and he is very much missed.